AN ACCIDENTAL ADVENTURE

WE DINE WITH CANNIBALS

Also by C. Alexander London

WE ARE NOT EATEN BY YAKS

AN ACCIDENTAL ADVENTURE

WE DINE WITH CANNIBALS

C. ALEXANDER LONDON

With art by JONNY DUDDLE

PHILOMEL BOOKS
AN IMPRINT OF PENGUIN GROUP (USA) INC.

To my sister, who first
made books come alive for me,
and to whoever does it for you.

PHILOMEL BOOKS
A division of Penguin Young Readers Group.
Published by The Penguin Group.
Penguin Group (USA) Inc., 375 Hudson Street, New York, NY 10014, U.S.A.
Penguin Group (Canada), 90 Eglinton Avenue East, Suite 700, Toronto, Ontario M4P 2Y3, Canada
(a division of Pearson Penguin Canada Inc.).
Penguin Books Ltd, 80 Strand, London WC2R 0RL, England.
Penguin Ireland, 25 St. Stephen's Green, Dublin 2, Ireland (a division of Penguin Books Ltd).
Penguin Group (Australia), 250 Camberwell Road, Camberwell, Victoria 3124, Australia
(a division of Pearson Australia Group Pty Ltd).
Penguin Books India Pvt Ltd, 11 Community Centre, Panchsheel Park, New Delhi—110 017, India.
Penguin Group (NZ), 67 Apollo Drive, Rosedale, Auckland 0632, New Zealand
(a division of Pearson New Zealand Ltd).
Penguin Books (South Africa) (Pty) Ltd, 24 Sturdee Avenue, Rosebank, Johannesburg 2196, South Africa.
Penguin Books Ltd, Registered Offices: 80 Strand, London WC2R 0RL, England.

Published simultaneously in Canada. Printed in the United States of America.
Edited by Jill Santopolo. Design by Semadar Megged. Text set in 11-point Trump Medieval.

Library of Congress Cataloging-in-Publication Data
London, C. Alexander. We dine with cannibals / C. Alexander London. p. cm.—(An accidental
adventure) Summary: All eleven-year-old twins Oliver and Celia Navel want to do is watch television,
but their explorer father takes them in search of El Dorado, the Lost City of Gold, and their long-lost
mother. [1. Adventure and adventurers—Fiction. 2. Explorers—Fiction. 3. Brothers and sisters—Fiction.
4. Twins—Fiction. 5. Television—Fiction. 6. Indigenous peoples—Fiction. 7. Rain forests—Fiction.
8. Amazon River Region—Fiction.] I. Title. PZ7.L8419Wg 2011 [Fic]—dc22 2010041993
ISBN 978-0-399-25488-8
1 3 5 7 9 10 8 6 4 2

CONTENTS

"I have already lived and enjoyed as much of life as any nine other men I know . . . if it is necessary for me to leave my bones in South America, I am quite ready to do so."

—PRESIDENT THEODORE ROOSEVELT

in a letter to Frank Chapman, ornithologist

1

WE ARE NOT EXPLORERS

CELIA NAVEL CLUTCHED the rope as if her life depended on it, although *her* life did not depend on it.

Her brother's did.

Even though she could no longer see him, Celia knew that her twin brother, Oliver, was hanging by his belt loops at the other end of her rope inside a deep, dark chimney that stuck out of the ground. The opening was overgrown with weeds, and the chimney looked like the top of carrot. Celia did not like carrots. In fact, Celia did not like vegetables of any kind.

Celia squeezed the rope so hard that her hands turned red and her knuckles ached. She hoped Oliver wasn't bumping into the walls. There could be bats. Oliver did not like bats. In fact, Oliver hated bats.

Celia leaned back, using all her weight to keep the rope from slipping, and she let it out slowly, hand over hand. Every time she moved her feet, the stone ledge crumbled a little more beneath her. She tried to remember what she had learned from the latest episodes of *The Celebrity Adventurist*, starring teen heartthrob Corey Brandt.

Corey Brandt's First Rule of Mountaineering: *Don't let go of the rope.*

Corey Brandt's Second Rule of Mountaineering: *Really, don't let go of the rope.*

Great, thought Celia. Now all I can think about is letting go of the rope.

The moon shifted behind high mountain peaks, casting strange shadows among the ruins that surrounded her. She squeezed tighter and continued lowering her brother.

The ledge on which she stood, and the chimney into which her brother was sliding, were part of a temple in the ruins of Machu Picchu, high in the Andes Mountains of Peru. The ruins contained old stone houses where no one lived anymore and grand temples where no one prayed anymore and hundreds of steps, towers, and terraces where no one did whatever people used to do on steps, towers, and terraces. During the day, it was a popular tourist spot.

Oliver and Celia, however, were not tourists. Tourists did not come to the abandoned city in the middle of the night. Tourists did not dress all in black. And tourists did not slide down overgrown chimneys into the ruins.

If we can call Oliver and Celia Navel anything other than Oliver and Celia Navel, we would have to call them explorers, though please don't tell them. They'd rather be called just about anything except explorers. They'd rather be called couch potatoes or dullards or dimwits or even tourists. Just not explorers.

Their parents are explorers. Most of the adults they know are explorers. They live on the 4½th floor of the Explorers Club in New York City. Explorers, they had learned through countless hardships and misadventures, were nothing but trouble. The kind of trouble Oliver was in right now, in fact.

As his sister lowered him down the narrow shaft, Oliver heard the snap of threads in his

belt loops. He hoped they wouldn't rip before he reached the floor. Oliver was an expert rope tier, thanks to the Saturday morning survival classes their parents had made the twins take. For every knot they learned how to tie, they were allowed to watch a half hour of cartoons. They quickly learned over a hundred knots and never missed a Saturday morning cartoon again.

Try as hard as he could, Oliver couldn't unlearn all those knots, so he was certain that his knot wouldn't break. However, his pants were not made for descending into ancient ruins. The belt loops were straining against his weight. He knew that his sister, high above, was straining too.

Oliver wasn't afraid of falling, though. He'd done a lot of falling off of things in his life. Earlier that summer, high in the mountains of Tibet, he had fallen out of an airplane, off a cliff, over a waterfall, and into an underground pit. How bad could a six-hundred-year-old chimney be? He was, however, afraid of a much slower and more painful end. He was afraid of upsetting the large *Heloderma horridum* hanging on to his back.

For those of you who are not herpetologists,

which is what an explorer might call a lizard scientist, a *Heloderma horridum* is a poisonous lizard found in Mexico and Guatemala that is roughly the size of a small dog. It is covered in greenish-brown bumpy scales, which give it its name. *Heloderma horridum* is Latin for "horrible armor," though the lizard is known in English as the beaded lizard. "Horrible armor" is a much more fitting name, however, for a lizard with such a grim expression and such a painful bite.

The one on Oliver's back was named Beverly. She wore a purple collar with a silver tag and liked eating Velma Sue's snack cakes. At least she and Oliver agreed on that. He patted his pocket to make sure he still had the snack cake he'd brought down with him—chocolate cake with bright red strawberry cream filling. Just in case he got hungry during the descent.

Beverly's claws were digging into his back and her head was resting on his neck. She kept flicking her tongue to remind him she was there. As if he could forget. If she bit Oliver with her venomous fangs, his face would swell, his nerves would twitch, and his whole body would be paralyzed.

Then he'd throw up his insides. He'd looked it up on the Internet. He really wished he hadn't. Too much information could be a really terrible thing.

Oliver, like most sensible eleven-year-olds, hated being bitten by poisonous lizards. It had happened to him before.

Twice.

He doesn't like to talk about it.

Five minutes earlier, he hadn't been nearly as worried about getting bitten by a lizard. He had been standing on the edge of the chimney with his sister and Beverly.

"Why should I have to go down there?" he had objected. He spit down into it to see if he could hear the *splat* when it hit the bottom. He couldn't. That took away all the fun of spitting off of things.

"Because I'm older," Celia explained.

"But we're twins!"

Celia sighed. She gazed out over the dark ruins. They were on the far edge of what was once a great stone city, separated from the rest of the ruins by a deep ravine. Whoever had built this strange chimney didn't want to make it easy for anyone to get to it. No wonder it hadn't been discovered in all the time that had passed since explorers first found Machu Picchu in 1911.

"Technically," she corrected her brother at last, "I *am* older. Three minutes and forty-two seconds older."

Oliver wasn't very good at details, especially the really important ones, like who was actually older. Celia believed that being three minutes and forty-two seconds older gave her some authority over Oliver in important decisions, such as what to watch on television and who should be lowered first down dark chimneys into ancient ruins at midnight. Oliver rarely agreed with her on either of those things.

"I can't go down there," he said. "I have the lizard."

"You can take her down with you. She'll scare away the bats."

"You think there's bats down there?"

"Don't be a sissy."

"Easy for you to say. You never go first." Oliver began tying the end of the rope onto his belt. "This is an injustice," he said while he tied. He could never win arguments with his sister, so he thought he'd save time by tying the rope while they were still arguing. He'd lose in the end anyway. He just tied his figure-eight knot and imagined he was tying his sister up with it. "I know my rights. I've seen more episodes of *Judge Baxter* than you have."

"Judge Baxter's a pet judge. He's on the Animal Network."

"It's still a courtroom. He's still a judge."

"He's a dog!"

"Dogs know what injustice is."

"Do not!"

"Do too!"

"Do not!"

"Do too!"

"Are we ready yet? We don't have all night!" a voice crackled over the walkie-talkie that Celia was holding.

Both of their heads shot up. Oliver and Celia looked across the ravine to a stone terrace in the main part of the city. There was a little man standing on it, surrounded by three large llamas. The man was the same height as Oliver and Celia, though he looked tiny next to the bored-looking llamas. He had an extravagant red mustache and a sour expression on his face, just like the lizard on

Oliver's back. In fact, the lizard belonged to this man. The llamas were rented.

The girl who owned the llamas sat on the stone steps of a temple a few yards away with her head in her hands, staring out at the jungle below. She hadn't said a word since she and her llamas had been hired. That was what the little man wanted. He'd hired the girl because her llamas were cheap, she knew the way to Machu Picchu, and she was mute. She couldn't say a word. The little man didn't want strangers talking about his business.

Like Celia and Oliver, the little man was dressed all in black, but his black outfit had a vest and a jacket and a black fedora. He would have been invisible in the moonlight if it weren't for his big red mustache and his bright red ascot. Even in the high Andes Mountains, the little man dressed to impress. The llama girl wore a colorful alpaca hat with long earflaps to keep her warm.

The twins stared across the chasm that separated them.

"*Well?*" the little man's voice crackled over the speaker again.

"You didn't say 'over.' We didn't know if you were done," Celia said. "Over."

They didn't need to listen through the speaker to hear the little man cursing. It echoed off the ruins and mountain peaks. We won't repeat the words he used here. Not all of them were in English, but their meaning was clear enough. The little man spoke into the walkie-talkie again.

"Will you please get down that shaft so we can begin, before I lose my temper and ship you both off to Siberia?" he said. *"Over."*

"I don't like Peru," Oliver said as he leaned forward, testing the rope. "Too many llamas." He was hanging over the edge of the chimney now. His sister began to lower him hand over hand. Oliver was still talking to her over his shoulder, his face pointing down toward the unknown.

"I don't like llamas. Too many letters. Why should they have two *l*'s? *Lama* with one *l* isn't much better . . . although *that* kind of lama tried to kill us in Tibet. I don't think I like llamas or lamas. At least lamas don't smell as bad as llamas. But still, I think the extra letters are confusing and not even . . ."

Oliver was still muttering to himself even after Celia could no longer see him. Soon she couldn't even hear him, but she could still feel him moving around at the end of the rope. She leaned back and held on tight. She'd made him go first and now Oliver's life was in her hands.

It was true that earlier that summer a man claiming to be a Tibetan lama had tried to kill them. He was really nothing more than a grave robber named Frank. He was eaten by a yeti. His partner, Janice, who had pretended to be a mountain climber, was still at large. That made Celia nervous. She didn't like having a grave robber bent on revenge wandering around at large. Although Janice the grave-robber-at-large was the least of her worries right now.

She had just heard a hissing sound from down in the chimney.

The hissing could have been bats, she thought. That would really make Oliver unhappy. But the sound could have been Beverly too. That would be much worse.

Like all *Heloderma horridum*, Beverly hissed when she was about to bite.

2

WE CAN'T EVER GET WHAT WE WANT

THE NAVEL TWINS, as we noted, were not sneaking into ancient ruins in South America in the middle of the night with a poisonous lizard because they wanted to.

They were there because their father had lost a bet with the little man wearing the fedora and the ascot, and explorers take bets very seriously. Because their father had lost the bet, the Navel twins belonged to the little man for the rest of summer vacation. They actually belonged to him for every vacation until they turned eighteen. Their father had made a very bad bet indeed.

The little man's name was Edmund S. Titheltorpe-Schmidt III, but he insisted that everyone call him Sir Edmund, which everyone was happy to do because "Titheltorpe-Schmidt the Third" was not easy to say.

Try it.

You'll be grateful he's called Sir Edmund, even if no one really believed that he earned the title of "Sir," which you can only get by being knighted, which means that you've done something noble and virtuous. And that you're British. Sir Edmund was neither noble nor virtuous. And he was not British. In fact, no one knew where he was from. Namibia? Uzbekistan? Dayton, Ohio?

What Oliver and Celia did know about Sir Edmund was that he was not to be trusted. He was rich and powerful and full of tricks.

Aside from being rich and powerful and full of tricks, he was, just like the twins' parents, a member of the Explorers Club, the most esteemed society of adventurers, explorers, daredevils, and globe trekkers in the world. The headquarters are in New York City, but the club has members on every continent, in every jungle outpost, and in every deep-sea trench. They've even had members walk on the moon.

Their father, Dr. Ogden Navel, was not only a member of the Explorers Club, he was the celebrated Explorer-in-Residence, which is why they lived in an apartment on the 4½th floor.

Their mother, Dr. Claire Navel, was also an Explorer-in-Residence at the Explorers Club, but she had not been "in-residence" for over three years. She'd gone to search for the Lost Library of Alexandria, which she believed had never been lost at all. She thought it had just been put away for safekeeping and forgotten for a few thousand years, like that cuckoo clock that belonged to your great-uncle Klaus in Bavaria that must be *somewhere* in the house, even if you can't remember where in time for the yard sale.

"Creation is persistent," Oliver and Celia's mother always said. "Nothing just vanishes without a trace."

Then she went off and vanished without a trace.

From that day on, it was just Oliver and Celia and their father in their apartment at the Explorers Club. And it could get lonely. Oliver and Celia were the only children allowed in the building, except for the occasional boy prince from Saudi Arabia or a visiting child-goddess from Kathmandu. They couldn't even invite their friends over.

Not that it mattered. They didn't have any friends. Their father was always taking them out of school to go on adventures around the world, to discover ancient ruins or isolated pygmy tribes or to search for their mother. All the kids at their last school thought they were weird or crazy or just plain liars.

Oliver and Celia wished they *were* lying.

They wished they were lying about the cursed birthday presents they got from Zanzibar or the fried scorpion cheesecakes they ate in Cambodia. Or the lizard bites. They also wished they were lying about how their mother had disappeared.

But they weren't.

Everyone thought that she had been lost, just like the library she'd gone looking for. It happened to explorers all the time. The history of exploration was a history of people getting lost. Sometimes they got lost looking for treasures or exotic animals and sometimes they were looking for lost places, like cities or libraries. Sometimes they were just looking for their car keys. The world was a big place and it was easy to get lost.

But earlier that summer Oliver and Celia's mother had suddenly shown up again.

She had lured them to a monastery in Tibet, high in the Himalayas. Sir Edmund had been trying to find her himself and had taken the twins prisoner to get to her. It was their mother who rescued them.

When she rescued them, she told Oliver and Celia that she was part of an ancient secret society. She told them that they were part of it too and that it was *their* destiny to discover the Lost Library. She told them they had to find it before Sir Edmund, or there would be terrible consequences. They even heard a prophecy from an oracle.

All that is known will be unknown and what was lost will be found.

Their mother couldn't explain it. Then she vanished again.

If they were part of this secret society and if they did manage to find the Lost Library of Alexandria, it would be one of the greatest discoveries in history, and they would be two of the greatest explorers in history. However, as we noted earlier, Oliver and Celia Navel did not want to be explorers. They did not want to go anywhere or discover anything.

They just wanted to watch TV.

Instead of being lowered into a crumbling chimney in ancient mountain ruins in the middle of the night with a poisonous lizard on his back, Oliver would have preferred to spend the entire summer in front of the television watching *Celebrity Whisk Warriors* or *Agent Zero* or *The Celebrity Adventurist*, where teen heartthrob Corey Brandt wandered into the wilderness with nothing but a knife and a handheld camera to see if he could survive. Oliver liked it. Adventure was fun when it was somebody else's.

Celia, whose hands were burning with the strain of the rope, felt the same way as Oliver, though she would have rather watched her favorite soap operas, like *Love at 30,000 Feet* or the Spanish channel's *Amores Enchiladas*. She also liked the talent shows, like *Dancing with My Impersonator*, although she stopped watching it when the Corey Brandt impersonator got kicked off for being too old and too tall and too not Corey Brandt. Oliver was glad. He hated dancing.

Celia was Corey Brandt's biggest fan, ever since *Sunset High*, where he starred as a dreamy high school vampire who had trouble in algebra class. She didn't like his haircut in *Agent Zero*, but she loved *The Celebrity Adventurist* because she got to see Corey Brandt defying danger and pursing his lips dramatically.

If they survived the rest of the summer as Sir Edmund's servants, their father had promised they could get cable television. While survival itself would be enough motivation for most reasonable people, Oliver and Celia needed the hope of hundreds of channels, video on demand, and high-definition broadcasting to keep them going.

They had already spent weeks with this mustachioed little man, traveling around South America, mostly visiting libraries and talking to old scholars about obscure subjects, like botany—the study of plants—and pogonology—the study of beards. Their boredom was indescribable and they still didn't know what he was looking for. And now there was only a week left until they'd have to start the sixth grade.

They did not want to start the sixth grade.

They did not want to climb into the ancient ruins of Machu Picchu.

They did not want to risk their lives for Sir Edmund because their father had lost a bet or get involved in another deadly adventure because their missing mother thought they were destined to discover the Lost Library of Alexandria. They did not want to get bitten by any lizards.

But as a great philosopher once said, "You can't always get what you want."

The hissing lizard on Oliver's back was about to make sure of that.

3

WE ARE BUGGED

BEVERLY'S HISS WAS as loud as a train whistle. For a second, Oliver thought he'd gone deaf. He felt Beverly's lizard breath on his neck and he froze. His sister must have heard the hiss too, because she stopped lowering him.

He didn't know how close he was to the ground, but he hung in the dark and squeezed his eyes shut. Sightless and soundless, he waited for the end to come. Any second, Beverly could slam her fangs into the back of his neck and that'd be it for Oliver Navel. He'd never see twelve years old. He'd never see sixth grade. He'd never see *The Celebrity Adventurist* holiday special. He wasn't ready to die.

"Okay, girl, calm down," he whispered. "Everything's fine. You don't need to get all hissy and bitey. Just stay calm."

"*Hiss*," Beverly answered.

"Are you okay?" Celia called down the tower. *Okay, okay, okay, okay*, her voice echoed around Oliver.

"I, um . . . ," Oliver shouted back up. *Um . . . um . . . um*, his own voice echoed.

"*Hiss*," Beverly hissed. *Hiss, hiss, hiss*.

Oliver felt the lizard's body tense and felt her head tilt back. She was about to strike.

"Oh no." Oliver gulped and squeezed his eyes shut tight again. He had always feared he'd meet his end from a lizard bite. "Do your worst, lady lizard," he whimpered, which he decided were pretty good last words, even if he only whimpered them. Heroes on television always had good last words.

Beverly's mouth opened wide. Her head shot forward like lightning and her jaws snapped shut with a sickening crunch.

"Ah!" Oliver yelled and tried to pull his neck away. He felt a flapping around his face and heard a loud screech. When he opened his eyes he discovered, much to his surprise, that he did not have a giant lizard attached to his neck. He hadn't been bitten. He turned his head and looked at Beverly clutching a vampire bat in her jaws. She blinked at him. The bat had been a millisecond away from biting Oliver in the face. As we know, Oliver hated bats.

"Are you okay?" Celia shouted down again, frightened for her brother's life.

"Yeah," Oliver called back up to her. "Just lower me faster, please!" He let out a breath and watched as Beverly gulped the vampire bat down her throat. "That's really gross," he told the lizard. "But thanks for catching it."

He could feel the lizard chewing next to his ear, which I will not describe. Some sounds are better left to the imagination.

At the top of tower, Celia started lowering the rope again. She wondered why her brother had screamed. He probably thought he saw something in the dark and got frightened. He really was such a wuss.

Oliver finally reached the ground. The moonlight pierced the dark in one single shaft of silver. He couldn't see much beyond it, which was fine by him. He'd hate to see a thousand more vampire bats hanging around. Beverly flicked her tongue at Oliver's neck. She probably wouldn't mind more vampire bats. Oliver, however, had work to do.

He tugged three times on the rope around his waist. His sister up above responded with three more tugs to show she had gotten the message. It was her turn to come down.

While he waited, Oliver pulled out his Velma Sue's snack cake and shared it with the lizard. He hoped his sister would be down soon.

Celia wondered for a moment how she would get down. She looped Oliver's rope around a rock behind her to act as a safety line and then looped her end through her legs to make a harness. She tugged it a few times to make sure it was sturdy and let out a slow breath. Corey Brandt always made this sort of thing look easy on television. In real life, rappelling down a dark chute in the middle of a jungle was not easy at all.

She put on her backpack and stood facing away from the dark hole. The moon slipped behind a cloud, like it was too frightened to watch. Celia's mother had climbed Mount Everest when she was seventeen years old. At eleven, Celia didn't even like to climb off the couch.

"I'm going down," she said into the walkie-talkie. "Over."

"Get on with it!" Sir Edmund snapped back, and she could see him jumping up and down with annoyance.

"Do you mean—?"

"Get on with it!" Sir Edmund's voice crackled. *"Over!"*

Celia smiled. She really enjoyed annoying the little man. Then she peered backward into the dark hole and let out a long breath. The first step was always the hardest. She leaned back slowly and sat down into her harness, hanging over the edge. One foot at a time, she began to walk down the inside of the wall, letting the rope out through her hands as she went. As she got more comfortable, she started to bounce away from the wall, soaring a few feet down through the air before landing on her feet again.

If one absolutely had to go into a dark pit in some ancient ruins, she thought, rappelling wasn't the worst way to do it. In under a minute, she was on the floor next to her brother.

"That was fast," said Oliver. "It looked a lot more fun than how I got down."

"It was okay," said Celia. She didn't want Oliver to think she'd had fun. He was always going on about injustice. "You've got snack cake on your face," she said, and then pulled out the walkie-talkie. "We're in," she said. "Over."

Oliver wiped his mouth.

Both children looked grimly up at the hole high above them. The rope hanging down was their only way out. It was sort of nice to get away from Sir Edmund for a few minutes, but they were kind of trapped in this hole now.

They turned on their flashlights.

"Tell me what you see," Sir Edmund's voice crackled through the heavy silence.

"You didn't say over. Over," said Oliver.

"Enough of that nonsense," Sir Edmund shouted through the speaker. *"When I am done speaking you will know it."*

"What are we looking for? Over," Celia asked.

"Don't worry about that," his voice crackled again. *"Just tell me what you see."*

They scanned their flashlights around the chamber.

"The floor is covered in little black kernels, like popcorn. Over," said Celia.

"*That is six hundred years of bug carcasses and dung.*" Sir Edmund laughed into the walkie-talkie.

"Wait—we're stepping on, like, dead bug bodies and um . . ." Oliver whimpered. He hated bugs.

"*Dung.*" Sir Edmund laughed. "*Beetle poop. It seems they gave the maid the last few hundred years off.*"

"That's disgusting!" said Celia, who had never swept up after herself. Someone always took care of cleaning and that sort of thing, though she wasn't sure who. Probably her father. Oliver had never given it much thought either. He didn't ask too many questions as long as he had clean underpants.

"Let's get this over with quickly," Oliver said.

He swept his flashlight along the walls of the room. They were covered in gold, with turquoise lines running through them like veins. The twins had never seen so much gold in their lives. They wondered if Sir Edmund planned to steal it.

At the far end of the chamber was a giant golden door. The door was decorated with a turquoise face made from thousands of tiny stones. Its teeth looked like the mountains around Machu Picchu, and images of dolphins and other sea creatures poured from its mouth. One of the doors had fallen a little open, just enough for an eleven-year-old to slip through. Oliver tried to tug it open wider, but it wouldn't move. He shined his flashlight through and his heart sank. The door led to a long tunnel.

Oliver really hated tunnels.

He looked back at Celia and she nodded at him.

"Oh no!" Oliver objected. "Why do I have to go first again? This is an injustice! I should sue! I should call Judge Baxter! I should—"

"There's a tunnel," Celia said into the walkie-talkie. "We can't see where it leads. Over."

"Don't be such cowards," Sir Edmund snapped. It was easy for him to be brave. He was safe aboveground with the llamas and the llama girl. *"Think of all the stories you'll be able to tell your little friends at school."*

School. Sixth grade. Now Celia was filled with dread too.

"We don't have any friends," said Oliver.

"What's down there? Over," Celia asked Sir Edmund. They waited in silence for his reply.

"You're entering the abode of the last Inca priests."

"Abode?" Oliver asked his sister. She knew all the vocab words.

"Home," she quickly replied.

"How do you remember all this stuff?"

Wally Worm's Word World," she said. "From when we were little. If you'd paid attention, you wouldn't have to ask all the time."

"I never liked that show. I hate puppets."

"What's wrong with puppets?"

"Who would want to learn vocabulary from a giant talking worm?"

"So you don't hate puppets. You hate worms."

"Whatever. I hate both."

"Well, there won't be any puppets in that abode," she said.

"Didn't the Incas perform human sacrifices?" Oliver gulped. He'd seen a movie where the priests tied people onto a stone altar and sacrificed them to their gods.

For a moment, Celia felt bad about making Oliver go first.

"Try not to step on any skeletons when you go through," said Sir Edmund. *"You never know what curses they might have left behind."*

Celia didn't feel that bad about making her brother go first anymore.

4

WE HAVE SOME HISTORY

"NEXT TIME," Oliver told his sister, "you're going first." He held his flashlight in his teeth like a pirate holding a dagger so he could use both hands to pull himself through the narrow opening in the doorway.

"Whatever," Celia said.

"I een in," Oliver said through the flashlight, which could have meant "I mean it" or "I'm eating." It was very hard to understand him with a flashlight in his mouth. He wasn't moving, though. Just staring at her.

"All right. Next time I'll go first," Celia finally agreed. Oliver could be really annoying when he pouted. Younger brothers were a pain, especially if they didn't think they were younger.

Oliver nodded and slipped into the tunnel. He wished he were home with the television. He wished he were safe on the couch. Heck, he thought, he'd even be okay with doing his summer reading!

The president of the Explorers Club, Professor Rasmali-Greenberg, had given Oliver and Celia each a book to bring with them to South America for their summer reading. The books were written by their parents, but Oliver and Celia hadn't even taken them out of their backpack. They'd been staying in luxury hotels. How could they be expected to read books when they had 218 channels to watch? Right now, Oliver would trade anything for a nice place to sit and read without any bats or tunnels or dark abodes. Beverly jumped off his back and scurried past him into the dark.

Oliver knew a thing or two about the Incas who had built this place because he had seen Corey Brandt in the made-for-TV movie *Sleepwalker 2: Inca's Revenge*, and what he knew was not comforting. And it wasn't just the human sacrifices.

There was a lot of garroting in that movie.

Garrote was a vocabulary word Oliver wished he *didn't* know. The garrote was a metal collar with a crank handle for tightening that Spanish soldiers used to strangle their enemies. Spanish soldiers were the first Europeans to discover the empire of the Incas in Peru. The soldiers were mostly uneducated brutes who had crossed the ocean looking for fame and fortune. They were called the *conquistadors*, which means "conquerors." The natives of South America were not happy to find themselves "discovered" by these conquerors.

The conquistadors conquered the Inca empire, garroted the emperor, and became the new rulers. They took all of the gold and silver that they could find and melted it down and shipped it off to the king of Spain. They liked all the Incan treasures, but they were not impressed with the oracles and the native religions, so they tore down the shrines, destroyed all the records, and renamed all the places. They didn't want to merely conquer the Incas. They wanted to destroy their culture completely.

But some things survived; stories told in whispers, secret places that the conquistadors could never find. Machu Picchu was one of those places. And this chamber, the secret home of the priests, was a place no one had seen since the last priest fled into the jungle hundreds of years ago.

When Celia finally squeezed through the door

and stood beside Oliver, it was a relief. He didn't like being alone with all that history.

Celia scanned the tunnel with her flashlight. "No creepy skeletons so far," she said as she nudged Oliver forward.

"There's always creepy skeletons," he answered her. "Didn't you see *Sleepwalker 2*?"

"There were no creepy skeletons in *Sleepwalker 2*. You're remembering it wrong."

"Am not," Oliver objected. "There were creepy skeletons all over that cursed temple they discovered. They'd been garroted."

"I never forget a Corey Brandt movie," Celia answered.

"Fine," Oliver said. His sister *was* obsessed with Corey Brandt. Maybe she did remember the movie better than Oliver. "If there's no creepy skeletons, that's good then, right? Maybe this won't be so bad."

"Not exactly," Celia sighed. "There were mummies. Lots and lots of mummies."

Oliver's heart sank. Now he remembered. The cursed temple in *Sleepwalker 2* was lousy with mummies. After he'd seen it, he couldn't look at a roll of toilet paper for over a month.

If you are keeping a list of the things Oliver hated, you might want to put mummies above bats and lizards and tunnels and the garrote. He *really* hated mummies. Celia felt the same way, perhaps even more so.

Even with Corey Brandt in the movie, there was nothing cute about mummies.

5

WE BATTLE BIODIVERSITY

THEY HAD TO CLIMB over broken stones and fallen pillars as they made their way down the hall. They stumbled and tripped over sheets of solid gold that had fallen off the walls. As they walked, their feet kept crunching on the dead bugs on the floor. They held their flashlights in front of them like magic wands. Celia heard a noise behind her and spun on her heel. She couldn't see anything.

Oliver would have asked what was wrong, but at that moment he couldn't speak. His face was suddenly covered in cotton candy.

At least it felt like cotton candy.

It wasn't cotton candy.

Celia froze where she stood and looked right at Oliver.

"Don't move," she said.

Oliver had just walked face-first into a large spiderweb and woken up the large spider that lived there. The spider did not appear to appreciate the abrupt end to her nap. She dropped from the shadows and landed directly on top of Oliver's head. He could feel her legs moving around through his hair. He felt sick to his stomach.

"What is taking you two so long?" Sir Edmund's voice crackled over the speaker. *"What have you found? Are you alive down there? Over? Over!"*

Celia ignored Sir Edmund and focused on her brother. She had to think clearly now. She had to remember everything she knew about spiders.

Her brother was the one who watched nature shows. She preferred soap operas and dramas. Anything with a good story and plenty of romance. How would that help her now?

"Celia," Oliver whispered through the strands of web covering his face. He stood stiff as a board.

"Yeah?" Celia whispered back.

"Is there a spider on my head?"

"I'm afraid so."

"Is it a big one or a little one?"

"I don't know. Big compared to what?"

"I guess compared to my head!"

"Yes, it's a big one."

Oliver gulped. "What's it doing?"

"It's moving around, like it's dancing," Celia explained.

Oliver turned pale, and not just because he hated dancing. The South American wandering spider was known to dance back and forth just before it attacked. He'd learned that on *Insect Files: Along Came a Spider*. He'd also learned that the South American wandering spider was the most venomous spider in the world.

"Beverly," Oliver whispered. "Where are you? You still hungry, girl? A little dessert after your bat? There's a yummy spider on my head. . . ."

Oliver couldn't believe he was actually *trying* to get the most poisonous lizard in the world to jump on his head, even if it was so it would eat the most poisonous spider in the world. This was not how he imagined his day would go when he woke up that morning.

Beverly, however, did not jump on his head. She had just eaten a bat and half a snack cake and she was scurrying around in the dark, crunching on beetle shells like they were popcorn. She was as happy as a *Heloderma horridum* could be. She had no desire to fight the poisonous spider on top of Oliver's head.

"Just stay calm," Celia told her brother. "I'll think of something."

Celia thought about her favorite soap operas. *Amores Enchiladas* was no help. *Love at 30,000 Feet* wasn't either. Why would there be spiders on a show about an airplane? Captain Sinclair once had an affair with a woman called the Black Widow, which was a kind of spider. She tried to poison his doughnut. That wasn't really helpful. What did *The Celebrity Adventurist* have to say about this?

Don't let go of the rope, she thought.

That was not helpful. She remembered an interview with Corey Brandt on *Celebrity Access Tonight*. He grew up in Idaho. He liked to swim. His astrological sign was Capricorn.

She pictured him sitting with the interviewer, slouched in his chair, a wisp of brown hair falling across his forehead. The freckle under his eye looking like a little teardrop. "I'm a normal guy, you know? I don't have a personal shopper. I don't hang out with supermodels. I'm afraid of heights."

How was that supposed to help her? Why couldn't celebrities say useful things in interviews? She didn't know what to do.

She *did* know that she hated standing in the dark thinking about TV shows that couldn't help her. She *did* know that this was a terribly dangerous place for two eleven-year-olds to be, and that if it weren't for their father's dumb bet with Sir Edmund or their mother's disappearance or the Lost Library of Alexandria, they wouldn't be there at all.

She thought about what her parents would do in this situation.

They would want to study the spider and think about why it behaved the way it did, and wonder what they could learn from it about *biodiversity*, which was just an explorer's way of saying "weird stuff in nature." She decided to do the opposite of what her parents would do.

Celia took a deep breath and then snatched the giant spider with her bare hands. In one swift motion, she tossed it to the floor and stomped it under her foot into a squishy mess.

"Ah!" Oliver screamed.

"It's gone!" Celia screamed back.

"Why did you do that?"

"Someone had to do something!"

"But that was the most poisonous spider in the world."

"Well, I didn't know that!"

"They're very rare!"

"Well, it could have killed you!"

"It could have killed you!"

"Well, it didn't."

"Sometimes you need to stop and think more," Oliver told his sister. She could be very impatient.

"Are you still alive?"

"Yeah."

"Then stop complaining and come on."

"There's some good news," Oliver added.

"What's that?"

"We've found the janitor's closet."

"The what?"

Oliver pointed his flashlight ahead of him. The hall opened up into a grand chamber and the far wall was covered with what looked like hundreds of colorful mops.

"We've found mops," Celia said into the walkie-talkie. "A room full of ancient mops. Over."

"It's a miracle!" Sir Edmund's voice boomed through the speaker. *"Go in, get a closer look!"*

"Is he going to want us to clean down here?" Oliver asked nervously. "I hate cleaning."

6

WE ARE NOT CLEANING UP

THEY SHINED THEIR lights around the room.

"Whoa," Oliver said.

"You're *sooo* good with words." Celia rolled her eyes.

Along the far wall, hundreds of thick bundles of colorful string were hanging on golden hooks, all the way from the floor to the ceiling. As they stepped closer, Oliver and Celia saw that the bundles were definitely not mops. Each thick cord of string had different colored strings hanging off of it, sometimes hundreds, and every string was filled with knots.

Oliver looked all the way up to the ceiling, which was decorated with a giant golden key, studded with sapphires and rubies. "It's that symbol," Oliver said. "Mom's symbol."

"The Mnemones," Celia sighed. "Of course. Why couldn't we just break into a normal Inca ruin?"

The Mnemones were the secret society their mother had told them about. *Mnemones*, for those of us who are not experts in phonics, sounds like "knee-moans," because the first *m* is silent. The *k* in *knee* is silent too. There's no good way to describe a secret society that doesn't use silent letters.

The Mnemones were an ancient society of scribes from the Library of Alexandria. Their symbol was a jeweled key with Greek writing beneath it. They were the scholars of the library, recording every book and prophecy and object in the ancient collection. They preserved all the knowledge in the world, examined it, studied it. They had known the Lost Library better than anyone.

Their enemies were a mysterious Council made of the most powerful people in Alexandria, who wanted to control the library for themselves. Somehow, in the conflict between these two groups, the Great Library of Alexandria went from being great to being lost.

Some scholars said it burned down. Some said

it was looted and then burned down. And some, like Oliver and Celia's mother, believed that it had been hidden and not burned down at all.

The Mnemones and the Council were now locked in an ancient and deadly race to find it again. That's what had led the twins to Tibet, and that's why their mother had not come home, and that's why Sir Edmund had brought them to South America.

He worked for the Council. He might even be its leader. They didn't know why he wanted to find the library so badly, but he was not the type of explorer who would donate his discoveries to a museum. His plans were certainly as selfish as they were mysterious.

Oliver and Celia couldn't imagine why anyone would want to find an old library so badly, but they were caught up in the race now. Between their mother's secret society, Sir Edmund's Council, and Janice McDermott, the grave robber bent on revenge, Oliver and Celia Navel found themselves wishing the Lost Library had just burned down two thousand years ago. Then maybe they'd be left alone. Then maybe their mother would come home.

Sir Edmund's voice crackled over the speaker. *"What do you see? Celia? Oliver? I swear if you don't speak soon, I will feed you to a llama!"* Oliver looked concerned.

"Relax," Celia said. "He can't feed us to anything while we're down here and he's up there."

"Do llamas eat people?" Oliver wondered.

"Llamas eat grass. How many nature shows have you watched?"

"Tons, but still . . . things are always weirder in the real world than on TV."

"We just see a lot of moppy, stringy things," said Celia into the walkie-talkie. She knew she couldn't tell Sir Edmund about the symbol on the ceiling. She wondered if he already knew. He'd sent them down there for a reason, after all. "Over."

"What is this place?" Oliver wondered. He went over and touched one of the bundles of string. Some of the knots were different colors and different shapes. From what he knew about knot tying, it would be very hard to tie so many different kinds of knots so many times. Why would someone do that?

"Look for one with gold on it," Sir Edmund said. Oliver and Celia scanned along the wall with their flashlights, looking at the different colors on

the strings. There were strings dyed blue and yellow and red. There were strings dyed turquoise and purple and black. There were strings dyed neon green and neon orange.

There was a burst of static and the walkie-talkie squealed with feedback. Celia let go of the button. More static came through.

"You're breaking up. Over," Celia said.

"The—gold—if—find the golden—," Sir Edmund's voice crackled.

"I can't understand him," Celia said. "Something about gold."

She put the walkie-talkie down and ran her hands through the strings.

"I found one with gold on it," Oliver said. He pointed up high toward a thick golden cord with more little strings hanging off of it than any other bundle. The other strings were every color under the rainbow, but the thickest one was made of shining golden thread.

"Climb up and get it so we can get out of here," Celia said.

Oliver just sighed. It wasn't worth arguing about with her. He never won. So he started climbing up, using the bundles of string for handholds.

Celia was studying the bundle in front of her. The cord was smooth and a little slick to the touch. She was running her hand along a knotted neon-green string, lost in thought. Her brow was wrinkled.

"I don't know what this place is," Oliver said, "or what it's got to do with Mom." His voice was strained with the effort of climbing. "But I wish they'd left a ladder down here."

Beverly was scurrying up the wall next to him. She seemed most comfortable when she was climbing. Not Oliver. He was exhausted when he finally got his hands on the golden cord about fifty feet off the ground.

"Got it!" he called back down happily.

Deserted—thirty—victorious," Sir Edmund's voice crackled over the speaker, though both twins were ignoring it now.

"Of course it would be the one all the way up here," Oliver said. "Why can't people ever be looking for things that are on the ground?"

"This isn't right," Celia said, still staring at the string in front of her.

"What? I can't hear you! Hold on. I'll be right down." Oliver pulled the golden cord off the wall.

It was really heavy with all the string. He couldn't imagine what Sir Edmund would want with it, but he knew better than to ask. Explorers were always looking for weird old things that made no sense, the older and weirder the better.

"Don't touch anything!" Celia suddenly screamed up at him. "We have to get out of here now! It's a trap!"

By then, however, it was too late. As Oliver pulled the heavy bundle of string off its hook, one of the strands pulled tight. He saw that it disappeared into a hole in the wall, while all the others hung loosely. He pulled it a little harder. There was a loud clicking sound.

"Uh-oh," he said. The giant key in the ceiling started to rotate, like it was unscrewing from the ceiling. It sent clumps of dust and stone falling to the ground as it turned. He put the golden cord quickly back on its hook, but it didn't help. A stone slab slammed down behind them, blocking their way out.

"Um . . . we've got a problem!" he yelled down at Celia, who was staring at the giant stone blocking their path. She wanted to yell at her brother but she didn't have time. She had to dodge chunks of falling rocks. Then the floor started to split open in the middle. As the key in the ceiling turned, the crack in the floor grew wider. Celia jumped off to one side to avoid falling in, but the crack kept growing. The floor was disappearing under the walls, like a rug being pulled out from under her. She was running out of floor very fast.

From where Oliver was hanging, high on the wall, he could see right down into the pit as the floor opened. It was about as a deep as a swimming pool, but they would never survive a fall into it.

"Oh no," he said as his worst fear came true.

He really hated mummies.

7
WE PLAY PEGGO

"CLIMB UP HERE!" Oliver shouted down at his sister.

Celia looked up at Oliver and then down at the pit in the floor. There were hundreds of mummies. They were wrapped in rotten cloth, with dark stones for eyes. Their lifeless mouths grinned up at the wall of strings and their lifeless eyes stared blankly ahead. Each of the mummies held a sharp spear in its wretched hands. If Celia fell into the pit, she'd be skewered on the spears like a marsh-mallow on a stick.

She rushed to the wall that was covered in strings, stumbling a little as she ran. The floor kept moving out from under her. Just as she was about to run out of floor and fall into the pit of mummies, she leaped into the air and caught onto a bundle of string. The floor disappeared underneath her. She looked down over her shoulder at the pit and realized that the only way to go was up. There were no safety ropes this time.

Celia started to climb. She wanted to get as far away from the mummies as she could. They still looked mummified for the time being, but if Celia knew anything about mummies it was that they never stayed dead for long. If there was a mummy on TV, it was sure to come to life eventually. It was like a law.

As she pulled herself up, she felt the string pull away from the wall and then stop. There was a hissing sound. She looked up for Beverly the lizard, but Beverly was climbing back and forth on the ceiling. The sound didn't come from her.

"Duck!" Oliver shouted.

Celia turned and saw a shining spear flying right at her. She swung out of the way like a monkey on a vine and grabbed another bundle of string just as the spear slammed into the wall where she had been. As her weight settled onto the new string, she heard another hiss and turned to see a spear shoot out of a mummy's skeleton hand. It was flying right at her. She let go and fell. The spear stuck into the wall again, just where she had been. She caught onto another bundle of string just before she fell into the pit. Again there was a hiss, and a spear was shot from a mummy's hand, aimed right at her.

"It's all booby-trapped," she said as she climbed up and out of the way.

"Keep moving!" Oliver yelled. "Climb toward me!"

Celia, who had spent more hours watching shoe commercials than playing on jungle gyms, found herself climbing and swinging like an acrobat from string to string, leaping and falling and catching on as spears shot at wherever she landed. She couldn't stay still for more than a second.

Her arms were tired, but she couldn't stop to rest. Every rope she caught onto set off a spear that was aimed right at it. The trap was designed so that you needed to use the ropes to climb when the floor pulled away, but the ropes made the spears shoot right at you. It might have been fun for a gymnast or a circus performer, but it was exhausting and deadly for Celia Navel. It was way too much like gym class.

Celia was swinging up one side of the wall and

down the other, dodging spears as she climbed and swung and jumped. Oliver knew his rope had set off the trap, but it didn't seem connected to a spear. He was safe where he was, so he reached out a hand and tried to catch Celia when she got close to him. She caught the rope right below him and pulled herself up, her face red and sweating. Just as their hands met, a spear shot between them and Celia let go so her brother's hand wouldn't be impaled. She fell.

"Celia!" Oliver yelled out in helpless agony, but his sister caught another bunch of string near the bottom.

As the rope hissed with her weight, she kicked her legs out behind her, using the string like a swing. She was flying through the air again, up and away, as the spear found its mark where her head might have been a moment earlier. As she flew forward, exhausted from her aerial acrobatics, she saw the shaft of a spear sticking out from the wall in front of her. She wrapped herself around it with a thud. It wobbled and shook, but it stayed in the wall.

The spears weren't connected to a trap, she realized. Only the strings. Celia hung from the spear while she caught her breath. She was relieved she hadn't been impaled.

"You okay?" Oliver called to her.

"The spears . . ." She panted. "The spears . . . playing Peggo."

"Peggo?" Oliver shouted. "Why are you talking about Peggo?"

Peggo was a game that people played on *Name Your Price*, an afternoon game show about guessing what things cost, like toilet paper and new cars. In Peggo, the contestant dropped a disc down a board covered in pegs so that it bounced around all the way to the bottom and the player won prizes depending on where it landed. Why his sister was babbling on about Peggo was beyond Oliver's understanding.

He looked down at his sister, slung like a rag over the shaft of the spear. Straight down below her, the cruel stone eyes of the mummies gaped upward.

"What do we do now?" Oliver called down.

"It's just like Peggo," Celia called up. "The spears are the pegs."

"And we're the little discs?" Oliver asked.

"That's right," Celia said.

"What about the mummies?"

"They aren't real mummies, Oliver," Celia said. "They're just part of this trap. They're like the robot bears at Super Fun Pizza Animal Jamboree."

"I hate those robot bears. Bears shouldn't play country music. It's just wrong. And the pizza there is rubbery."

"I know, but as long as we use the spears and don't put any weight on the strings, we won't set off the trap again. Though we have to figure out how to get out of here."

"Now all I can think about is pizza."

"I think I see a way out," Celia said.

She pointed at the key on the ceiling that had spun around when the floor opened up. It was like a big screw. Now that it had been loosened, they could see a spiral staircase on the back of it. That was their way out. Beverly was hanging upside down next to the stairs, waiting for Oliver and Celia. The only problem was that the stairs were in the middle of the ceiling over the pit of mummies below.

"We'll need more pegs to climb up there," Celia said. "And it's your turn."

"What? Why? No!"

"I said when we came down here that I'd go first the next time, remember? You made me promise. And I did. Look at all the spears I put in the wall."

"You didn't do it on purpose," Oliver said. "That's not fair."

"I went first. Now it's your turn," Celia said. "You've had longer to rest anyway."

"Hanging up here isn't resting!"

She just glared at him. He sighed. His sister was right. She was *always* right. Even when she was wrong. That's what it meant to have a sister who was older by three minutes and forty-two seconds.

Oliver let go of the rope he was on and fell a few feet to the next one down. He caught it with his right hand. There was a hissing sound when he grabbed on and he saw a spear firing out from one of the mummies down below. He whipped his legs out behind him and dodged the spear, swinging away to the next rope as the spear hit the wall. He swooped and swirled along the wall, up and down like an acrobat.

Beverly's head moved from side to side as she watched. Celia called out to him as he raced along.

"Duck down . . . swing left . . . now to the right . . . no, your *other* right . . . now leap!" she called. If it weren't for her, Oliver would have been shish kebab.

Oliver caught another spear stuck in the wall just above Celia. He was out of breath and soaked with sweat, but happy he was still alive. The wall of colored strings looked like a pincushion.

"Okay," Oliver said. "Peggo."

"Great job," Celia said. "Now we've got to climb."

His arms felt like floppy noodles at that point. "If this were TV," Oliver said, "there would be some heroic music and they'd cut away and we'd be safe already."

"Well, it's not TV, so we have to climb." Celia started climbing. Oliver groaned and followed.

High above the blank stares of the long-dead mummies with glistening spears, Oliver and Celia climbed from spear to spear, all the way up to the ceiling. When they reached the top, Oliver balanced himself on two spears and took a big leap to the giant key. He caught on and his legs dangled in the air. For a moment he thought he might fall, but he pulled himself up. His sister jumped after him, and he caught her arms and pulled her onto the stairs. She was very happy she had a younger (by three minutes and forty-two seconds) brother.

"I don't think Sir Edmund's going to be happy with us," Oliver said. "I don't think we found what he was looking for."

"I think somebody else beat us to it," Celia said. "That was no ancient trap."

"How do you know?"

"*Fashion Force Five*," Celia explained, as if it were obvious how a fashion reality TV show explained it all. "I'll tell you later," she added.

Beverly climbed onto Oliver's back and the twins started up the winding stairs, side by side.

8

WE BORROW A LLAMA

SIR EDMUND WAS STANDING on a pile of rubble, scolding the small girl as she packed up the llamas.

"Hurry up! Put that in the bag . . . here . . . here . . . *aquí* . . . *sí*? You don't even speak Spanish, do you?" He was muttering and stomping in frustration, although he didn't offer to help the girl. "Useless! Useless!" he shouted. "Why am I always stuck with children? If they aren't dumb TV-addled brats, they are mute jungle people with no sense at all!"

The girl just kept packing bags onto the llamas, but her eyes glowed angry under her long dark hair. If he'd been paying attention, Sir Edmund would have noticed that she could understand every word he said.

Oliver and Celia came out from underground onto a terrace above them. They were sweaty and dirty and tired. The sky was growing brighter in the east. Tourists would be arriving soon with their fanny packs and their digital cameras. Sir Edmund wanted to be out of there before anyone spotted him.

"Lousy, lazy kids . . . too much TV! . . . I should have known . . . couldn't even find their way through an Inca ossuary," Sir Edmund was muttering.

"What's an ossuary?" Oliver whispered to Celia.

"It's a final resting place for human bones," Celia said.

Oliver stared at her.

"*Wally Worm's Word World.*"

"But how do you remember it?"

"You make a rhyme, like *Bones are scary, lock 'em in the ossuary.*"

"*Ossuary*'s a strange word to be on a kids' show."

"Don't blame me," Celia said. "I didn't write it."

One of the rented llamas tilted its perky ears toward Oliver and Celia. It was copper colored with long scraggly fur that looked like dreadlocks. It showed its teeth in a giant llama grin.

"*Heuuurrr,*" it bellowed. The little girl looked over toward the twins and smiled.

"Oh, be quiet, you ridiculous-looking creature, or I'll make dog food out of you," Sir Edmund scolded, but the llama stepped away from him and trotted up toward Oliver and Celia.

It looked back at Sir Edmund and added a quick "*heuuurrr,*" with another grin.

"You two!" shouted Sir Edmund when he saw Oliver and Celia. "What are you doing still alive? You stopped answering me. I had hoped you did so because of an untimely demise, not because you were being rude! I should have known you'd do something like this."

"Like what?" Celia said.

"Survive," Sir Edmund answered. "With nothing to show for it."

"We *nearly* died," said Oliver.

"You led us into a trap," said Celia. "What was in that place?"

"All you had to do was tell me what you saw." Sir Edmund ignored her question.

"We saw a bunch of string," Celia said. "Like old mops."

"Those weren't mops," Sir Edmund said. "They were *khipu*."

"Key-poo?" Oliver asked. "Is that like bug poo?"

Celia shrugged. This time she didn't know the word either.

"Khipu," Sir Edmund said, "is an ancient Incan form of writing using colored knotted strings where each color and each knot mean something. Every 'mop,' as you call it, is an entire book of knowledge. So far, no one has been able to decode them. The Spanish destroyed most of them when they conquered the Inca empire."

"But the Spanish never found Machu Picchu," Oliver added. *Sleepwalker 2* was coming in handy. "They never knew about all those key-poops."

"Khipu," Celia corrected him.

"That's what I said. Key-poops. So you were here looking for old books." Oliver threw his hands in the air. "Another library! What is it with explorers and libraries?"

Sir Edmund picked at his fingernails. He was wearing shining silver cuff links that showed an image of a scroll wrapped in chains: the symbol of the Council.

"One of those khipus could have told us the way to El Dorado if you hadn't been so careless," he said. "You've heard of the Lost City of Gold, I assume?"

"We've heard of it," Celia snapped at Sir Edmund. "So you want gold now?"

"What I want is none of your business," Sir Edmund grunted.

"Well, those were fake khipus down there," Celia said. "That wasn't a real Incan library or whatever."

"Nonsense," Sir Edmund answered, but there was doubt in his voice.

"It was a trap."

"Rubbish. The Inca didn't make booby traps. You've seen too many movies."

"The Inca didn't make these traps," Celia said. "They were new."

"And how do you know that, young lady?" asked Sir Edmund.

"How *do* you know that?" asked Oliver.

"*Fashion Force Five,*" Celia said. "And *Celebrity*

Fashion Crimes. Neon colors weren't even invented until the twentieth century. The Incas couldn't have used those colors. When I saw the neon strings, I knew that the place was fake."

Sir Edmund thought about it a moment.

"You aren't lying to me, are you?" he asked.

"No," Celia said. "I never lie."

Oliver gave her a knowing look.

"About TV," she added.

"You've told me everything?" Sir Edmund asked.

"Yes," Celia lied. She hadn't told him about the big key in the ceiling.

"All right then," Sir Edmund said. "That is enough. You are free to go."

"What?"

"I am done with you for now. You may return to your home at the Explorers Club."

"But we're in the mountains," Oliver said. "In Peru."

"Please be quiet. I have to think now. I said you are free to go."

"But—"

"You may take a llama."

"But—"

"That is all."

The llama with the dreadlocks nudged Celia with its nose and bared its teeth again.

"*Heuuurrr*," it told her. "*Heuuurrr*."

"Where is that llama girl?" Sir Edmund said, looking around. "Where did she go?"

The girl was nowhere to be seen. Sir Edmund called out to her, though he only knew her as Llama Girl. He got no answer. She was gone and hadn't left so much as a footprint.

"I should have known she'd do something like this. The natives are terribly unreliable. At least she left her llamas. I can get a good price for these two back in the capital."

"You're just going to steal her llamas?" Celia asked.

"They are *my* llamas now and you better get moving with that one," said Sir Edmund. "I believe you have school in about a week and llamas do take their time getting from place to place."

"But what about the girl?" Celia looked around, hoping the girl would pop out and demand her llamas, maybe yell at Sir Edmund.

"Oh, don't worry about her. . . . I'm sure she's just run home for some cannibal feast."

"Cannibals? Like eating people?" Oliver looked nervously to the jungle on the slopes of the mountain.

"Yes, Oliver, like eating people. The natives in this part of the world are savages. They lack our civilized refinements." He laughed. "Now go. Take that llama before I change my mind and leave you for her friends to make a stew out of."

Sir Edmund turned away from them and looked back across the mountains at the chimney they had gone down hours before. Celia kept looking around at the ruins, wondering if the llama girl was all right, wondering if cannibals were lurking in the shadows. Why had the girl run off like that?

"Oh," Sir Edmund called out to the twins. "And take Beverly with you. She's fond of Oliver for some reason, and I'd hate to upset her. I'll get her back from you in the city."

Beverly licked the back of Oliver's neck, which was her way of saying, "I am happy about this turn of events. It is most fortunate for our relationship and I will treasure your company."

Oliver thought her tongue felt like sandpaper.

"You know what I really hate?" he said as he climbed onto the llama's back with Beverly.

"Let me guess," Celia said as she climbed on behind him, trying not to disturb the poisonous lizard. "Is it llamas now?"

"No," Oliver said. The llama started to make its way along the rocky slope between a giant temple and the ruins of a small stone house. Oliver scratched it behind the ears. "They're actually kind of cute. Cuter than yaks anyway."

He looked back at Sir Edmund, who was writing frantic notes in a small book and shaking his head. He didn't even turn to watch Oliver and Celia go. "Explorers," Oliver said. "I really hate explorers."

9

WE ARE DISAPPOINTED WITH DAD

OLIVER AND CELIA'S FATHER, whom Oliver did not hate, in spite of his being an explorer, had cleaned up their apartment on the 4½th floor of the Explorers Club for the twins' homecoming, though one could hardly notice.

Piles of paper sat next to the sofa and the top of the fridge was stacked with old leather books. It was hard to find a place to put all of his maps and charts, because their apartment was filled with knickknacks and bric-a-brac and tchotchkes, which is just another way of saying a lot of stuff from all over the world. They had shards of thousand-year-old pottery and a knife made from the bones of a whale and a fanged spirit mask of the Liberian chimpanzee devil.

When Oliver and Celia's parents traveled, they never brought back T-shirts.

Dr. Navel had put his rolled-up maps in the corner between a collection of traditional Zulu fighting sticks and the Cabinet of Count Vladomir, which was a medieval torture box. He had shoved his charts into the freezer, where there was plenty of room. He cleaned all the crumbs from under the couch cushions and even discovered loose change from five different countries that no longer existed. He didn't want to throw it out, so he put it back under the cushions.

He cooked Celia and Oliver's favorite dinner: macaroni and cheese. He didn't even do anything weird to it, like adding spicy Mexican habanero chilies or fried Bolivian grubs. Dr. Navel couldn't imagine eating macaroni and cheese without spicy Mexican habanero chilies or fried Bolivian grubs, but he was willing to do anything for his children. So he made boring old mac and cheese, and he set up snack tables in front of the television.

Normally he would not allow them to eat dinner in front of the television, but it was their first night back and it was his bet that had made them

Sir Edmund's slaves. So he was prepared to let them eat in front of the TV.

He stood in front of the couch next to the steaming bowls of cheesy noodles and listened for their footsteps on the stairs. When he heard them coming, he was overwhelmed with excitement and flung open the door.

"Welcome home!" he shouted, beaming at his children. Oliver and Celia stared back at him with exhausted faces. Beverly was asleep on Oliver's head.

"We took a taxi from the airport," Celia said.

"Oh yes, of course!" their father answered, fumbling to find his wallet. "I would have picked you up myself, but there was a problem with the Mbuti diorama at the museum and then I had to cook dinner, and that took a few tries, and I wasn't quite sure when your flight landed, and I . . ." He was still muttering excuses as he rushed past them to go downstairs and pay the taxi driver.

Oliver and Celia came right inside and flopped down face-first on the sofa. Beverly took over Dr. Navel's armchair in the corner.

"It must have been extraordinary to see Machu

Picchu at night!" Dr. Navel exclaimed as he came back into the apartment. "Some scholars say the city was planned as an earthly mirror to the Milky Way."

Then he saw the twins, sound asleep without having touched their dinner. He was dying to hear about Oliver and Celia's adventures—how they had nearly been impaled in Machu Picchu, how they had ridden a llama all the way to the capital city and caught a flight home on a military transport, and most of all, what they had learned about their mother and the Lost Library. Even though they had been gone for over a month doing hard labor for a very bad man, their father seemed to think it had been an enriching experience for them, like summer camp.

He wondered if he should let them sleep. He imagined they would be hungry, though. They had to eat. He coughed. He coughed again. Neither of them moved. He tried to move Beverly off of his chair and she hissed at him.

"Careful," Oliver muttered with his face still pressed into the sofa cushion. "She'll bite." Then he went back to sleep.

Dr. Navel had one more idea. He turned on the

TV. A rerun of *Dancing with My Impersonator* was on.

"Sorry, Corey Two, but you've been voted off!" The host smiled as a sad Corey Brandt impersonator wept into his hands. "The audience thought you were too tall and too old and too *not* Corey Brandt. Better luck next time!"

Celia and Oliver sat bolt upright.

"Is that—?" Oliver asked.

"Do we have—?" Celia wondered.

"Did we get—?" Oliver tried again.

"Is it cable?" Celia blurted.

Oliver smiled and shoved a forkful of mac and cheese into his mouth.

"I . . . um . . ." Dr. Navel blushed and rubbed the back of his neck. He looked down at the floor.

Oliver froze with his spoon in his mouth.

"Ooo sed wud et cahoo!" Oliver shouted through his mac and cheese, which either meant "You said we'd get cable" or "Who said we're in cahoots?"

The second one wouldn't make much sense, but Dr. Navel looked like he was thinking about it.

"You didn't get us cable, did you?" Celia flopped

back onto the couch cushions. She knew what her brother had said.

"You . . . *gulp* . . . promised!" said Oliver, swallowing.

"I know, guys," their father apologized. "I meant to call the cable company, but I got distracted trying to figure out where your mother might have gone after she left Tibet. I kept finding this strange key symbol and the summer just got away from me."

Their father didn't know about the Mnemones or what that mysterious symbol meant. Their mother thought it would be safer if he didn't know. If Oliver and Celia had thought about telling their father before, now they were really angry and definitely weren't going to tell him anything.

"This is an injustice!" Celia exclaimed. She nodded at her brother.

"Uh-huh!" he shouted. "Injustice!"

"I know, I know." Dr. Navel shook his head. "It's just that I was so close to finding your mother. I thought that maybe, while you were gone, I'd find her again and she'd be here by the time you got back. I found three new species of dust mites living in old books, but nothing to help me find your mother. I'm sorry."

"Do not fear, dear Navels!" Professor Rasmali-Greenberg exclaimed as he burst into the apartment.

Professor Rasmali-Greenberg was the president of the Explorers Club and one of the most famous explorers in the world. He was considered a prince in several countries, a god in others, and had been banned from ever visiting the state of Minnesota again.

He was a very large man, and he had the world's largest collection of ties with ducks on them. Today, he was wearing a green one with orange ducks on it. He was also wearing a ring with a jeweled key on it. He was a Mnemone, just like their mother.

"Anticipating your return, I took the liberty of scheduling an appointment with the cable company to come tomorrow between the hours of ten a.m. and midnight. If all goes well, you will have cable TV installed while you are at school. Is that all right?"

Oliver and Celia considered this for a moment.

"Fine," Celia said, scowling.

"Fine," Oliver said, scowling too.

"Now, please tell us what you learned in South America," the professor asked, flopping his considerable bulk on the couch between Oliver and Celia. "Did you—ahem—do the summer reading I gave you?"

"Well, we meant to, but—," Celia began to make an excuse.

"You didn't read the books I gave you?" the professor cried.

"We were a little busy with spear-shooting death traps and stuff," Celia said.

"This is terrible. It was not supposed to happen like this at all." He stood again and began pacing back and forth, rubbing his fingers on his forehead like he had a terrible headache. "Oh dear . . . oh dear. I'm so sorry. So sorry."

"What's the matter, Professor?" Dr. Navel asked.

"Children, you really should have done your summer reading. It would have saved you no end of difficulty."

"What are you saying?" Dr. Navel asked again.

The professor grabbed their backpack from behind the couch and rummaged through it.

"Hey, that's ours!" Oliver objected, but the professor ignored him and pulled out two small books: *A History of the Great Scribes of Alexandria* by Claire S. Navel, PhD, and *A Guide to South American Flora and Fauna* by Ogden Navel, PhD. These were the books the professor had given them to read before they went off with Sir Edmund, that they hadn't so much as taken out of the bag.

He opened the *History of the Great Scribes* to reveal that every page was the same. Every page had one sentence typed neatly in the center:

DON'T TOUCH THE MOPS.

Then he opened the *Guide to South American Flora and Fauna*.

"Apologies, Ogden," he said as he showed that the book was hollow. There was a hole cut into where the pages should be, and from the hole he pulled out a small plastic game with little pegs and discs: Peggo Deluxe Travel Edition.

"Huh?" Oliver said.

"Huh?" Dr. Navel said.

"You knew about that death trap!" Celia shouted.

"I tried to warn you. I tried to help. I thought you'd at least open one of these books out of curiosity."

"But we aren't curious about anything!" shouted Oliver.

"Why didn't you just tell us?" said Celia. "Why do explorers always hide the important stuff?"

The professor just shrugged. It was like asking why tigers have stripes.

"How was travel Peggo supposed to help?" Dr. Navel asked. "I'm terribly confused."

"I had been informed that Edmund would go to the abode of the last priests of the Inca sooner or later, and I thought that maybe, if I could warn you, you'd be safe. He, of course, would not be. Sadly, I underestimated your dislike for reading."

"You were *informed*?" Celia asked.

"I did not get to be president of the Explorers Club because of my tie collection, you know. I have informants all over the world," the professor answered.

"But we were nearly killed!" Celia shouted. "Couldn't you have *informed* us?"

"Well, Celia, I thought I had. I thought children loved summer reading. I was obviously mistaken."

"Excuse me," Dr. Navel interrupted. "Could someone please tell me what is going on?"

"Your children are upset because I accidentally almost killed them with spear-throwing mummies in a death trap," the professor said. "But I had a good reason."

10

WE CHANGE CHANNELS

CELIA COULDN'T BELIEVE her ears.

"A death trap?" Dr. Navel asked. "Why?"

He almost accidentally killed his children all the time in the far-off places of the world, but he was their father. He wasn't so sure he liked it when other people almost accidentally killed his children.

"I thought I could free them from Sir Edmund," Professor Rasmali-Greenberg said. "And in the process, protect the Inca's Itinerary."

"What's that?" asked Oliver. Celia glared at him. "I mean . . . whatever," he added and turned toward the TV.

Celia turned up the volume. She didn't want to get caught up in another quest for another artifact and she didn't want Oliver getting caught up either. They had sixth grade to worry about, and no cable television, and no mother, and that was enough for two kids to handle. No more mysteries. No more adventures.

The Celebrity Adventurist had come on. Corey Brandt was standing in front of a giant redwood tree.

"Last week we learned that quicksand isn't all that dangerous as long as you don't panic. We also learned the hard way not to eat wild mushrooms off the ground. Today we're leaving the ground altogether to learn what it takes to survive for a whole week in the treetops of a giant redwood forest." He smiled and patted the thick trunk behind him.

"How would anyone get stuck in the treetops of a giant redwood forest for a week?" Professor Rasmali-Greenberg wondered aloud, interrupting his own train of thought.

"Shh," Celia snapped. She was happy just looking at Corey Brandt's smile. He didn't need to make any sense. Oliver thought Corey Brandt might just be the coolest guy in the world. His new show was reality TV. He wasn't acting. He wasn't using a stuntman. It was just Corey Brandt on his own, in the wilderness with a camera and his wits, and he was about to climb a really big tree.

"Professor . . . the Inca's Itinerary?" Dr. Navel said.

"Ah yes, well, some time ago I found myself in Machu Picchu, investigating the myth of El Dorado, the Lost City of Gold."

Celia turned up the volume on the TV. She didn't want to hear this nonsense. She knew that an itinerary was a plan for a journey, and she didn't like the sound of that. Journeys and investigations were bad news for Oliver and Celia Navel. And lost cities were even worse.

"It was there that I discovered a room of hidden khipu . . ." The professor had to raise his voice to talk over the television.

Celia turned it up again.

"*These trees are the killer whales of the arboreal world. I've never felt more unsafe!*" Corey Brandt was hugging the high branch of a tree, straining to tie a rope around his waist. His hands were shaking. The camera cut to a close-up. "*Remember, the first rule of thumb for any survival scenario: Try not to hurt your thumb.*"

"**I believe one of the khipu,**" the professor

had to shout over the television, "**was the Inca Itinerary, hidden from the Spanish Inquisition in Machu Picchu.**"

"**Were you able to break the code of the khipu?**" Dr. Navel shouted over the television.

"**I was not. I took it with me and left this trap in its place. But the golden cord implies the path to El Dorado might be contained in its—**"

Celia turned the TV up again. "***Being tangled in vines is like being stuck in quicksand,***" Corey Brandt told his audience, while he was tangled in an impossible mess of vines. "***If you panic and squirm, you make it worse.***"

"**CELIA!**" Dr. Navel turned to his daughter.

"What?" Celia asked, smiling innocently. Oliver mirrored her smile. They knew exactly how to drive their father insane.

"Could you *please* turn down the television?"

"Of course," Celia said as she turned down the television. "Could you please not involve us in any more deadly adventures? We have sixth grade starting tomorrow."

"Don't you want to know anything about this place?" their father pleaded as the TV volume went down. His shoulders slumped and his glasses slid down his nose. "It nearly killed you. Aren't you at all interested in knowing why? Aren't you interested in anything other than TV? Don't you want to find your mother?"

"Maybe Mom doesn't want to be found!" Celia snapped at her father, startling everyone in the room. "Maybe she cares more about old libraries and lost cities and weird mysteries than she does about us!"

Celia turned her back to the TV again and crossed her arms. Oliver started to speak but stopped himself. Celia glowered at him, boiling with anger. Oliver's lower lip quivered.

"We have school tomorrow," Celia added, and looked at the floor.

"School, right . . ." Their father let his voice trail off. He pushed his glasses up the bridge of his nose and kept his gaze fixed on the back of Celia and Oliver's heads.

"Perhaps we should adjourn to the Great Hall," the professor suggested after a very long silence.

"Yes . . . adjourn . . . ," Dr. Navel said, still looking at his children. He followed Professor Rasmali-Greenberg out of the apartment. Just as he reached the door, he turned back and spoke to Oliver and Celia. "Make sure you brush your teeth and go to bed when your show is over. And"—he cleared his throat—"I . . . you know . . . I think that . . ." He rubbed his hand along the door frame, searching for the right words to say. "I'm sorry for everything that's happened. I love you."

"Love you too," the children said absently as they stared at the screen. Corey Brandt was trying to catch a squirrel in a trap made of dental floss, but neither of the twins was really watching.

When they were alone, Oliver spoke.

"The professor just thought he was trying to help. He thought he would get Sir Edmund with that trap."

"Well, we don't need his help," Celia said. "His kind of help is bad for our life expectancy. I'd like to reach twelve."

"Do you think the professor will tell Dad about the Mnemones, and, you know, our destiny?"

"I don't know."

"Do you think he has that khipu Sir Edmund was looking for?"

"I don't know," Celia said again.

"Do you think Mom is in El Dorado?"

Celia just shrugged. She was still staring at the screen, but there were tears on her cheeks.

"Do you really think Mom won't ever come back?"

"I don't know!" Celia snapped. "Okay? I. Don't. Know!"

She was fed up. Oliver's curiosity was just the kind of thing that would send them off on another adventure, and adventures always ended up with missed television, lizard bites, and a lot of disappointment. Some things stayed lost for a reason, Celia thought. There wasn't any point in looking for things that didn't want to be found.

"Listen," she said. "The more we know, the worse things *always* get for us."

"But what were they talking about? What's an itinerary?"

"It's a plan for a trip, Oliver! A trip! An adventure! Do you really want to know more than that? The last time you wanted to know something, we got thrown out of an airplane into Tibet . . . by our own mother. You want to do that again?"

"She was trying to protect us."

"So was the professor, and look how that went."

"I mean, *The Celebrity Adventurist* is almost

over. There's nothing on TV now anyway. We might as well . . ."

Corey Brandt was rappelling down a giant redwood on a rope he'd cut from tree bark in a harness padded with leaves. It made Celia think about when she rappelled down that chimney in Machu Picchu. She wondered if Corey Brandt would be impressed that she knew how to rappel.

"I'm going to look," Oliver said, and he picked up the remote control. He started to press the buttons in different combinations. The channel changed to a commercial for snack cakes. Then to another.

"Do you even remember how to do it?" Celia asked.

"Just gimme a second."

"You're doing it wrong!" she said, and reached out to grab the remote. "If you're going to make us do this, at least do it right!"

"Hold on, I almost got it!" He kept pressing buttons and the channels kept flipping between commercials.

The TV blared: "Velma Sue's snack cakes, now in lemon-ginger cream!"

And then: "Our cakes are wholesome because the towns that make them are wholesome. Try a Velma Sue's snack cake today."

And: "This is not your grandmother's snack cake!"

"I heard that Velma Sue's snack cakes blow up if you put them in water," said Oliver.

"That's just a myth," said Celia. "You can't believe everything you hear."

"I saw it on the local news," Oliver said.

"Then it's definitely not true," said Celia as Oliver kept flipping from commercial to commercial. Beverly blinked at the TV. She liked Velma Sue's snack cakes as much as Oliver did.

"Just give me the remote!" Celia lunged for it, and just as she did, Oliver pulled the remote away so that Celia ended up smacking him in the face.

"Ouch," he said.

"Your own fault."

Oliver rubbed his cheek where she'd hit him. "It worked, didn't it?" He pointed at the TV screen.

WELCOME TO TABLET 2.0, the TV screen read. THE COMPLETE CATALOG OF THE GREAT LIBRARY OF ALEXANDRIA.

This was the souvenir their mother had given them the last time she left them, back in Tibet. It wasn't a T-shirt and it wasn't a knickknack or bric-a-brac or a tchotchke. It wasn't a fanged spirit mask of the Liberian chimpanzee devil.

It was a universal remote control that could access the complete catalog of the Lost Library of Alexandria—every book and scroll and mysterious treasure that had been hidden there since the library was founded over two thousand years ago. Right on the TV screen.

They had only opened it once before they had gone off to South America with Sir Edmund, but their mother had told them that the catalog would help them. They'd need it to find the Lost Library and she gave it to them to keep it safe. It also worked on any TV, which was a plus.

"So what do we look for?" Celia asked.

Oliver typed in the letters for "El Dorado" and pressed enter. A little cartoon man in a toga appeared and tapped its foot while the request was processed.

Suddenly, the toga man frowned and a message appeared on the screen.

ACCESS DENIED.

Oliver frowned and pressed some other buttons. The message repeated itself.

ACCESS DENIED. ACCESS DENIED. ACCESS DENIED.

"What?" Oliver wondered aloud. "It's broken."

He pressed more buttons. Suddenly the screen went dark. After a second, Corey Brandt appeared again, standing at the base of a giant tree.

"So remember," he said. "If you want to battle the giant redwoods, you'll need nerves of steel, eyes like lasers, and a copy of *The Celebrity Adventurist* companion photo book, on sale this spring."

He winked at the camera and it cut to the credits.

Oliver and Celia stared at their TV.

"Well," Celia said at last. "So much for the catalog."

"I guess." Oliver couldn't hide his disappointment.

"Whatever," said Celia. She couldn't hide her happiness. No more catalog in their remote meant that maybe there was no more destiny, nothing they could do to find the Lost Library. Maybe they could just be normal for a little while.

"There's a bright side," she told Oliver to try to cheer him up.

"What's that?"

"We'll get cable TV tomorrow."

Oliver smiled. He could argue with his sister about a lot of things, but never about cable television.

11

WE GET SCHOOLED

IT WAS THE MOST STRANGE and terrifying thing Oliver and Celia had ever seen.

Although they had endured many terrors in their eleven years and they had seen many strange things, from giant yetis to psychic yaks, nothing compared to what they saw before them at this moment.

Children screamed.

Furniture tumbled.

Paper flew through the air.

A *miasma*—which is what Wally the Word Worm might call a really stinky smell—of sweat and perfume filled the air. A *cacophony*—which is what Wally the Word Worm might call a lot of noise—shook the walls. Children of all different shapes and sizes darted from place to place like nervous lizards.

This was Mr. McNulty's homeroom five minutes before the start of the first day of sixth grade.

When Mr. McNulty—whose name was written on the blackboard—saw Oliver and Celia standing frozen in the classroom doorway, he waved them in.

"Don't be afraid!" He smiled. He was a big man, built like a football player, and his smile took over most of his very wide face. "We thrive on creative chaos here!" He stood up on his chair, which creaked under his weight. "It is my pedagogical approach!"

"Pedagogical?" Oliver whispered at Celia.

"I think it has something to do with feet." She shrugged.

"I see you have a lizard," said Mr. McNulty.

"Oh yeah, I have to watch her until—um," Oliver started to answer, trying to explain why he had a large beaded lizard on his back, but the bell interrupted him.

"Ladies and gentlemen, please take your seats so I can take the attendance!" Mr. McNulty called out. His voice boomed around the room, and all the kids sat down.

Oliver and Celia shuffled in. There were no

seats together. Celia sat in the back corner, which meant that Oliver had to take the last seat, way up front. He hated sitting in the front. Teachers called on you more and other kids thought you were a suck-up.

"Hey," a red-faced boy in a baseball jersey next to Oliver whispered. "What's with the lizard?"

Beverly flicked her tongue at the boy.

"Well, I have to look after her until Sir Edmu—," he started to answer, but Mr. McNulty interrupted.

"Welcome to the sixth grade!" he said. "I am your homeroom teacher, Mr. McNulty. We'll start the roll call. Please raise your hand when I call your name and announce in a loud, clear voice one thing you learned over the summer. Ready? Angstura, Greg."

"Present!" The boy next to Oliver raised his hand and said, "I mean . . . um . . . I learned how to throw a curveball."

"Excellent!" Mr. McNulty said. "Bessemer, Jill."

A girl toward the back of the room raised her hand and told everyone how she had learned how to do her own makeup. One of the boys said he'd learned how to beat every video game he owned. The girl right next to Celia talked about reading over thirty books. One by one, the sixth graders answered.

"Hey," Greg Angstura whispered to Oliver. "Can I touch your lizard?"

"I wouldn't," Oliver whispered back. "She's kind of, you know, like . . . poisonous."

"Yeah, right," Greg said.

"Navel, Celia."

"Here!" Celia said.

"And?" Mr. McNulty asked.

"And what?"

"What did you learn this summer? One thing."

"I dunno. Nothing, I guess."

"Nothing? Did you do anything special this summer?" Mr. McNulty was not going to let Celia off the hook. She didn't like all those eyes looking at her.

"I'm going to pet it," Greg whispered to Oliver.

"Don't do it!" Oliver whispered back.

"I dunno," Celia said. "Just normal stuff. We went to Tibet. We fell out of a plane. We watched *Love at 30,000 Feet*. Some witches and some explorers tried to kill us. Then we went to South America and our father's boss tried to kill us to protect some mops or something. Corey Brandt has a new show."

The class laughed, although Celia wasn't sure why. Corey Brandt's new show was really good. At least four girls had Corey Brandt's picture on their notebooks.

"Celia," Mr. McNulty said. "You should write short stories when we get to that in English class. But for now, why don't you just tell me one thing you actually learned this summer, okay? No make-believe."

The class laughed again. Celia was getting annoyed.

"I guess I learned never to trust adults," she said, looking right at her teacher.

Mr. McNulty's smile froze on his face. He blinked a lot.

"Fine," he said at last. "We'll just have to work on that. Navel, Oliver."

"*Hiss!*" Oliver said, and the class gasped.

It wasn't Oliver who hissed.

It was Beverly.

And the next thing anyone knew, the giant lizard had jumped from Oliver's back and landed on Greg Angstura's face.

"Ahhh!" Greg Angstura screamed.

"Ahhh!" Oliver screamed.

"Oh crud." Celia groaned and rushed forward to help her brother pry Beverly from the boy's face.

At the front of the room, Mr. McNulty fainted. Celia wondered if that's what he meant by his pedagogical approach. The other students jumped up on their chairs and screamed. Celia started to wish they'd been homeschooled.

12

WE KNOW OUR LIZARD

PRINCIPAL DEAVER LEANED back in her chair and studied the Navel twins over the rim of her reading glasses. Her office was tidy. Papers were stacked neatly in piles and weighted with antique paperweights. Her books were organized by color and size. A shiny bronze bust of Teddy Roosevelt sat on top of the bookshelf, gazing down at the room.

Principal Deaver was a small woman, but she made up for it with her severe haircut and an expression to match. In fact, she looked a lot like Teddy Roosevelt. And she made it clear that she was not to be trifled with.

"I am not to be trifled with," she said.

Beverly sat in a cage on the windowsill behind the principal, watching the scene with focused lizard eyes. Or she was asleep. It was hard to tell with lizards.

"I have been around the block a time or two," Principal Deaver said. "I'm no spring chicken," she added, as if Oliver or Celia thought she might be.

In truth, they had seen talking yaks and met a man who called himself a lama. Principal Deaver could have been a spring chicken, whatever that meant. Usually, when someone denied something without being asked, it meant that they were probably hiding the truth.

"In all my years as an educator," she continued, "I have never seen a first day of class like this one. What do you have to say for yourselves?"

"I told him not to touch the lizard," Oliver said, staring at his feet.

"Mr. Rondon, our custodian, was forced to put aside his normal duties to find a cage for that thing."

Mr. Rondon grunted. He stood behind Oliver and Celia in a crisp blue uniform. He was completely bald, with thick black eyebrows and large, powerful hands. He had very broad shoulders, like a bodyguard. A few dark lines of a tattoo peeked above the collar of his shirt. He made Oliver and Celia a little nervous.

"Her name's Beverly," Oliver said. Celia shushed him. Oliver never knew the right time to keep his mouth shut.

"Please tell me," the principal continued without acknowledging Beverly's name, "who thought it was a good idea to bring a poisonous lizard to the first day of school?"

"I didn't have a choice," Oliver said.

"Young man"—Principal Deaver leaned forward and laced her fingers together—"there is always a choice. *Always!*" She slapped her desk to make her point. Oliver and Celia stared blankly at her. Adults could be so theatrical sometimes. Behind them, Mr. Rondon cracked his knuckles. *That* made the twins shudder.

"Ma'am." Celia cleared her throat. She had decided to defend her brother, even though she could have stayed out of the situation altogether. She'd been in the back of the classroom, after all. She had her own problems with all those kids laughing at her. But Oliver was her brother. "Oliver thought it would be good for show-and-tell. He

loves . . . um . . . science and stuff. He was just trying to embrace . . . the . . . uh . . . pedagogical
approach."

Principal Deaver raised her eyebrows at Celia.
So did Oliver. Mr. Rondon let out a slow breath.
Beverly shifted from claw to claw, though it probably had nothing to do with the conversation. She
was just a lizard.

"Well," the principal said at last. "That is an
admirable idea, Mr. Navel. I am glad you think so
seriously about the method and practice of teach-
ing, but in the sixth grade we do not do show-and-
tell. You are very lucky that young Mr. Angstura
was not seriously harmed during the incident. You
both may return to class. Mr. Rondon shall keep
this lizard in his custodian's closet until the end
of the day."

"But she's poisonous," Oliver explained. "She
only trusts me."

"I take fine care. *Heloderma horridum* is fine
lizard, is no problem," Mr. Rondon said.

"I'm not worried about Beverly," Oliver said,
crossing his arms. "It's you I'm worried about. I
don't even like lizards."

"*Scientia potentia est.*" Mr. Rondon smiled. He

had a thick accent in English, but he seemed to speak Latin effortlessly. "It mean 'knowledge is power.' You must know your lizards. Is no problem."

"Don't worry about Mr. Rondon," Principal Deaver said, looking at the custodian suspiciously. "He seems to know his lizards."

Oliver and Celia turned to see that he was smiling.

"You may pick your lizard up from him at the end of the day. I do not suggest you bring it back to school tomorrow," said Principal Deaver, and dismissed the children. Mr. Rondon winked at them as they left the room. The dark curls of ink on his neck bulged as he gave them a reassuring nod.

"Thanks for the quick thinking," Oliver whispered to Celia as they made their way down the empty hallway.

"What are older sisters for?" Celia answered.

"But we're twins!"

When they returned to their classroom, Oliver and Celia were met by angry stares. The only smiles in the room came from Corey Brandt's picture on the girls' notebooks. There were now two open seats in the front of the room and the seats had a wide space around them, like a moat.

Mr. McNulty had a small bandage on his forehead. He eyed the twins nervously.

"Come in and take your seats," he said without any of the friendliness he'd shown that morning. Oliver glanced over at Greg Angstura, who pulled his chair farther away.

"Sorry," Oliver mouthed.

"You're dead at recess," Greg hissed back.

No one talked to Oliver and Celia for the rest of the morning, although they talked about Oliver and Celia behind their backs the entire time.

"Freaks," whispered Annie Hurwitz.

"Weirdos," said Stephanie Sabol.

"Lizard people," said just about everyone.

That one stung Oliver particularly hard. It wasn't even *his* lizard!

Finally, recess came, and the twins hoped to be left alone to mind their own business.

"Sixth-grade recess," Mr. McNulty explained to the class as they lined up to go outside, "is a time to reinforce socialization and cultivate interpersonal relationship skills."

The class stared back at him, dumbfounded.

"Sixth-grade recess is structured play," he explained, and led the class down the hall toward the double doors that led to the playground.

"What's structured play?" Oliver asked his sister as they followed the line outside.

"I think it means Mr. McNulty tells us what to do."

"So it's just like class, only outside?"

"Oh no," Celia said, squinting out at the blacktop in the glaring sunlight. "It's going to be much worse."

13

WE WOULD RATHER FACE LIONS

WHEN A YOUNG BOY reaches maturity, the San Bushmen of the Kalahari Desert send him into the dry savannah on his first antelope hunt. He faces hunger and thirst, and while he hunts for antelope, a pride of lions might be hunting him. Young men of the Satere-Mawe people in Brazil wear gloves filled with bullet ants, and must dance for ten minutes while the ants inflict their hands with hundreds of painful bites.

These are rites of passage that signal a transition from childhood into adulthood, and cultures all over the world have different ones. Some of them seem brutal and violent to outsiders. Some of them are hard to understand.

Middle school has its own rites of passage. The

most brutal, violent, and hard to understand of these is called dodgeball.

Celia and Oliver did not like dodgeball. Celia and Oliver might have preferred the lions of the Kalahari or the bullet ants of Brazil to facing Greg Angstura on the blacktop at recess.

"Oliver," Celia said as the class split into two teams with a row of red rubber balls placed in a line between them. "Remember the spears. We can dodge anything."

"Hold on!" Mr. McNulty shouted. "Team change! You and you, trade places."

Celia looked to her left and looked to her right. Mr. McNulty had pointed at her. She had to go over to the other team. She would have to play against her brother.

"I . . . um . . . ," she said.

"Go on! You're holding up the game."

Celia's shoulders slumped and she made her way across to the other side.

Mr. McNulty blew one quick blast on his whistle and the kids raced for the balls in the center of the blacktop. Oliver and Celia stood frozen in place, helplessly staring at each other. Dodgeball had begun. It was kill or be killed.

Greg Angstura whipped a ball sidearm at Oliver's head. Should he go left? Should he go right? He wavered. He waffled. At the last moment, he ducked. The ball sailed over him and smacked right into Jill Bessemer's face.

"Ow," she groaned, burying her face in her Corey Brandt T-shirt.

"Out!" Mr. McNulty blew his whistle and hooked his thumb to the sidelines. On both sides boys and girls were falling down with the smacking sting of rubber on flesh. Greg Angstura was a demon. He raced from side to side, taking kids out, firing rubber balls like the thunderbolts of Zeus.

Celia stood toward the back, sidestepping balls as they flew her way. Very few did. Greg was dominating the court, and it looked like her team would win. Except that Oliver had also moved to the back of the court and was sidestepping balls as they came his way. The boy who beat all his video games went out. Annie and Stephanie went out. Oliver was the only one left on his side of the blacktop, sweating and panting and leaping from side to side. The other kids watched him from the sidelines with blank stares, just like the mummies in Peru. This all felt a little too much like the fake Inca death trap. What twisted mind invented these sorts of tortures?

"Try to catch something!" Mr. McNulty pleaded. "Play!"

Greg raced toward the line in the center of the court and hurled a ball at Oliver with one hand. Oliver jumped and let it sail between his legs. As he landed, Greg swung another ball out from behind his back and it sailed right at Oliver's nose.

"Watch out!" Celia shouted.

"Ahhh!" Oliver shouted and put his hands up to protect himself. There was a loud *thwack*, and then silence.

Oliver had caught the ball.

"Out!" Mr. McNulty blew his whistle and hooked his thumb to the sideline for Greg to leave the court.

"You helped him! That's cheating!" Greg yelled at Celia. She just shrugged.

As Greg moped over to the sidelines, he scooped up a ball at his feet and, in one rapid motion, flung it at Oliver, who was still staring at the ball in his hands. Greg's throw struck him right in the ear with a *gong*! He wavered and waffled on his feet.

He went to the left. He went to the right. He fell onto the blacktop with a *plop*.

"Hey! That's cheating!" Celia yelled and ran up behind Greg Angstura, who was laughing at how Oliver fell down.

He was still laughing when Celia's fist hit him square in the face. It was his turn to hit the pavement. Celia was the only one on the blacktop left standing.

"Out! All of you! Navels! Angstura!" Mr. McNulty yelled and blew his whistle again and again. "To Principal Deaver's office! *Now*!"

"But—," Celia objected.

"Ugh," Oliver groaned, still lying on the ground.

"Ugh," Greg Angstura groaned, also still lying on the ground.

And just like that, recess came to its brutal end.

Principal Deaver was still at her desk when Oliver and Celia trudged back in. Half of Oliver's face was red from where it met the blacktop. Greg Angstura had a black eye. Celia's face was intact, but her sense of justice was wounded.

Sixth grade, she had decided, was nothing but a series of unfair punishments and cruel rituals. Like most things, it seemed like a lot more fun on television.

"I am not happy to see you both again," the principal said. "And Mr. . . . um . . ."

"Angstura," Greg said.

"Yes, Mr. Angstura." Principal Deaver looked at his face. "I think you should go to the nurse to have your eye looked after while I speak to these two."

"Yes, ma'am," Greg said as he left the room again. He stuck his tongue out at Oliver as he went.

"Hey!" Oliver started to shout, but Celia put her hand on his leg to stop him. They were in enough trouble already.

"Navels." Principal Deaver sighed. "Do you know who Theodore Roosevelt was?"

"There's a statue of him in the Natural History Museum," said Oliver.

"He was the president of the United States," said Celia, rolling her eyes at her brother.

"He was. He was also an explorer, much like your father. He led the first expedition to navigate the River of Doubt, a river in the Amazon rain forest. His son Kermit joined the expedition and played a pivotal role in its success. Father and son worked together, and now the River of Doubt is named after them, the Roosevelt River. There is no more Doubt. The greatness they achieved as explorers is due to one thing: Teddy Roosevelt's commitment to physical fitness."

"You mean, like, gym class?" said Oliver.

"I do," said the principal. "He believed that a mind could be healthy only if the body was healthy. They were part of a system and one could not be strong unless the other was strong."

"Okay," said Celia, not sure what the principal was trying to say.

"Your performance today has been weak," said Principal Deaver.

"So . . . you want us to lift weights?" Oliver asked.

The principal sighed and rubbed her eyes. "My school is like the Roosevelt expedition, parent and child working together to discover the Golden City of Knowledge. I am like the parent. You are like the child. And you are not strong enough to accompany my expedition."

"We don't really like expeditions," Celia tried to explain. "We're sort of indoor kids."

"It's a metaphor, Celia." Principal Deaver sighed.

"I think you mean a simile," Oliver added. "When something's *like* something else, it's a simile, not a metaphor." Celia's jaw dropped as the principal's face tightened. Oliver just shrugged at her. "What? I know stuff too."

The principal studied the twins in silence for some time and then her face cracked into a forced smile. She started writing on a piece of paper on her desk. "I think two weeks should do it," she said at last.

"Two weeks should do what?" Celia asked.

Principal Deaver handed Celia a note on school stationery.

"Give that to your father," she said. "We will call to let him know you are coming."

Celia looked down at the note. Of all the injustices she and Oliver had thus far faced, this was perhaps the worst injustice yet.

Oliver and Celia were being suspended for two weeks.

....

"You can't suspend us on the first day of school!" Celia objected.

"Celia, you have hit another student. Oliver nearly killed that same student with a lizard. I believe I *can* suspend you for two weeks and I believe I just have. You are the weakest part of my expedition! How's that for a metaphor, Oliver?"

Oliver shifted nervously in his chair. He hadn't meant to offend her.

"You may take your lizard from Mr. Rondon before you go." Principal Deaver went back to looking at papers on her desk and Oliver and Celia knew their meeting was over, along with their first day of sixth grade.

Everyone else was in class and the hallway was as silent as a tomb.

Actually, as the twins knew all too well, tombs are rarely silent. There are bugs buzzing and spiders chewing, and lizards hissing and occasional death traps. One could more accurately say that the empty school hallway was as silent as an empty school hallway. Nowhere else in the world is there such an eerie silence.

"Who names his son Kermit?" Oliver wondered.

"An explorer," said Celia with a roll of her eyes, pulling her brother along.

The door to the custodian's closet was still closed when Oliver and Celia got there. Their backpacks were weighed down with notebooks and textbooks they wouldn't use for another two weeks.

They couldn't hear any movement on the other side of the custodian's door.

"Maybe we should come back another time?" Oliver said. "I mean, if this were a horror movie, there would be a creepy body on the other side of this door and the moment we discovered it, it would start a whole chain of horrible events that would end with one of us getting eaten by cannibals."

"Yeah, but if this were a comedy, we'd find Mr. Rondon dressed up like a giant baby or something. Or, like in a soap opera, he'd be in there crying for his long-lost brother."

"And then we'd have to help find his brother and it would start a whole chain of horrible events that would end with one of us getting eaten by cannibals."

"That doesn't happen in soap operas."

"Well, it could."

"Well, you have to get Beverly," Celia said.

"I know, but—wait . . . what? *I* have to?"

"She's your lizard."

"She's Sir Edmund's lizard."

"Still. Your responsibility."

Oliver sighed. The injustices would never cease.

He knocked on the door. No answer.

"I tried. Let's go home," he said.

"Try the knob," Celia said.

Oliver tried the knob and the door opened. It creaked.

"Of course it creaks." Oliver groaned. "It always creaks just before something terrible happens." He closed his eyes and pushed the door open, wondering what it would feel like to be eaten.

"Hello," Mr. Rondon's voice boomed happily.

"*Gurrrlp,*" Beverly said, which was a completely new noise for her. Oliver opened his eyes to see Beverly on Mr. Rondon's lap. The custodian was petting her like she was a small dog. He set her on the floor carefully.

"Come," Mr. Rondon said. "Quickly, quickly." He ushered the twins into his little closet and closed the door. There was a shelf filled with cleaning liquids and a cart with a giant trash can on it and a lot of supplies and a big sink and an entire wall covered with mops. "I am sorry you had trouble. Now we hurry, hurry, hurry."

"What are you talking about?" said Celia, impatient.

Mr. Rondon turned and rummaged through the mops hanging on the wall until he found the one that he was looking for.

"Aha!" he said, and smiled. "All okay."

He turned around holding a brightly colored mop that the twins immediately knew was not a mop at all. For one thing, it had no handle, and for another, all the strings were different colors and they all had knots tied in them. They all hung from a thick cord made of gold.

"A key-poop," Oliver said.

"Khipu," Mr. Rondon corrected him, smiling.

"Okay, now really," Celia demanded. "What is going on here?"

Mr. Rondon opened the collar of his shirt to reveal the tattoo on his neck: an ancient key with all kinds of crazy writing in squiggly letters around it, ancient Greek letters, to be precise.

The symbol of the Mnemones.

"You take khipu," he said. "You will need. For the Lost City of Gold."

"Um, *what*?" said Oliver.

"We don't want it," said Celia, crossing her arms.

"You need soon. Your mother say so."

Celia uncrossed her arms.

"Wait, you've seen our mom?" Oliver exclaimed. "When? Where?"

"She come to me, just a few—"

With a *bang*, the door burst open and Principal Deaver stood in the hallway. Next to her stood a large school safety officer, even larger than Mr. Rondon. The officer clutched his walkie-talkie like a weapon. Mr. Rondon quickly shoved the colorful bundle of string into Celia's backpack. The principal didn't seem to notice.

"I believe it is time for you to be going," the principal said. "Your suspension has begun." She gestured at the lizard and Oliver picked Beverly up in his arms like he was carrying a baby. He grunted under the lizard's weight. She didn't scurry onto his back this time, so he had to strain his arms to carry her out of the closet.

"Mr. Rondon," the principal said, looking at the custodian's open collar. "I never did notice your tattoo before. How very . . . *interesting*. Perhaps you can tell me about it in my office." She looked down at Celia. "You may go," she said. "Go straight home. Your father is expecting you."

She rested her hand on Celia's shoulder to guide her out and Celia saw, much to her dismay, a golden bracelet on Principal Deaver's wrist inscribed with a picture of a scroll wrapped in chains.

14

WE AWAIT OUR PUNISHMENT

OLIVER AND CELIA didn't speak. People gaped at them as they walked the streets of New York City in the middle of the day with a large lizard. They were thinking about what had just happened.

Everywhere Oliver and Celia went, it seemed, they were doomed to find explorers, and not all of them were friendly.

Celia wondered why there were explorers working in their school, and why she and Oliver would need this unreadable guide to El Dorado "soon." Oliver wondered how much it would hurt to get a tattoo like Mr. Rondon's and wondered what country he was from.

Both of them wondered where their mother was. When had she talked to Mr. Rondon? Why hadn't she come back to them?

They stopped outside the grand arched doorways of the Explorers Club.

"Do you think we'll be grounded?" Oliver wondered.

"I hope so," said Celia.

"Me too," said Oliver.

If they were grounded, they'd get to stay in the apartment for the next two weeks with cable TV. No adventures. No school. No dodgeball. Just the couch and some snack cakes and *The Celebrity Adventurist*. Heaven.

As they stood on the street, the doors to the club opened, and there stood Dr. Navel, looking very serious.

"Celia, Oliver," he said. "Come inside."

The children stepped into the building. They stood in the lobby in front of a giant old globe that had been given to the club by a crazy Scottish duke. Most of the countries on it were either in the wrong place or didn't exist anymore. Some of them probably never existed. Oliver was always tempted to spin it, but no one was allowed to touch the globe. Dozens of animal heads watched them from the walls with lifeless, glassy eyes.

"I received a telephone call from your principal," Dr. Navel said. As he spoke, an explorer dressed in scuba gear came down the stairs and rushed past them, running like a penguin in flippers. He popped out on the street and jumped into a waiting taxi. Dr. Navel continued.

"Celia, violence is never the answer to your problems," he said. "I do not approve of you hitting other children. That being said, your suspension could not have come at a better time!"

He smiled and wrapped his arms around the twins.

"What? You aren't mad?" Oliver asked. "But we got suspended from school on the first day! Aren't we grounded? Why aren't we grounded?"

"We demand to be grounded!" said Celia.

This was an unexpected and unfortunate turn of events.

"Why ever would you be grounded?" Dr. Navel asked.

"Oh, I don't know . . . because we got suspended from school!" Celia said.

"Oh, school can wait! There will always be more of it. I have a surprise for you! Come along!" He turned and rushed up the stairs. Oliver and Celia looked at each other. Beverly leaped off

Oliver's back and raced up behind Dr. Navel. The lizard seemed to like surprises.

Oliver and Celia did not.

Their father's surprises never went well for them.

"Do you think we have cable now?" Oliver asked.

Celia just sighed and pushed her brother up the stairs ahead of her.

The stairs grew narrower and narrower as Oliver and Celia climbed to the 4½th floor. The carpet grew more and more threadbare. At one point, a small staircase branched off the main one, which led them to their apartment. A large moon rock sat on a shelf just above the door. It always fell when the door slammed too hard, scattering bits of precious moon dust onto the carpet.

The twins came inside and looked immediately to the television, hoping their surprise would be a glistening new cable box. They couldn't wait to catch up on *Agent Zero*, *Love at 30,000 Feet*, and of course, *The Celebrity Adventurist*. They were fairly sure that video on demand was the greatest human achievement since the moon landing.

But there was no cable box.

There was no cable guy installing a cable box.

There was, however, an unknown figure sitting on their couch with his back to the twins.

"Where's the cable box?" Celia asked, slamming the door behind her. They heard the moon rock hit the ground outside with a thud.

"You promised!" Oliver added, ignoring the man on the couch, who did not turn around.

"I have something so much more exciting for you than cable," said Dr. Navel.

Oliver and Celia deflated like day-old birthday balloons. This was turning into the worst day ever. Certainly, their father was about to introduce them to some famous deep-sea diver or long-distance camel racer or crazy-eyed shaman or some other person he thought was fascinating, who would bore the twins with hours and hours of stories and photos and artifacts.

"I'd like to introduce you to my new friend, just back from the northern wilderness," Dr. Navel said as he stepped into the hall to put the moon rock back on its shelf. Celia could barely contain her groan. "He's traveled a very long way to be here," Dr. Navel called back into the apartment.

The figure on the couch stood up and Celia

rolled her eyes, which she immediately wished she hadn't done.

Because she was standing face-to-face with the teen heartthrob and star of *Sunset High*, *Agent Zero*, and *The Celebrity Adventurist*, Corey Brandt.

15

WE ARE RECEIVING VISITORS

"YOU MUST BE CELIA," Corey Brandt said, smiling. His eyes seemed to sparkle and his hair fell in shining brown wisps across his forehead. He put his hand out for Celia to shake.

"Uh, um, uh," Celia said, staring at Corey Brandt with her mouth hanging open and her arms hanging loose at her sides. He was taller in person than she'd imagined him.

"I'm Oliver," Oliver said, grabbing the actor's hand and shaking it wildly with both his hands. "I love *Agent Zero*. My favorite episode is when you're trapped on the roof of the Hashimoto Bank building, wrestling a panther, and you use your prep school tie to ride a power line like a zip cord and then you jump that speedboat into a private pool party so you can take Melissa St. Germain to the prom, but she tries to kill you and everyone thought you were slow dancing but you were really fighting and she was really an assassin from the Nori Crime Syndicate, and that was really, really awesome, but I wonder if you use a stuntman, because I once fell off this cliff and went over a waterfall and it really hurt and I just don't think I could do that every day for my job like you do, if you don't use a stuntman, but I just think it's really cool even if you do, but it would be even cooler if—"

"Hi," Celia finally said, interrupting her brother.

The room fell quiet and everyone stared at each other.

At that moment, Professor Rasmali-Greenberg came out of the bathroom, drying his hands on the bright yellow duck tie he was wearing.

"Ah, Celia, Oliver, you are home at last. I trust the sixth grade is going well?"

"Um," Oliver started.

"They were suspended for two weeks," Dr. Navel explained.

"Excellent!" The professor clapped. "Well done!"

"We didn't *do* anything," Celia objected. She looked at her brother in disbelief. Things were getting very strange indeed. The adults were all happy they had been suspended, there was no cable in the apartment, and Corey Brandt was standing in their living room.

"I had to leave regular school when my acting career took off with *Sunset High*," Corey Brandt said. "I didn't miss it, you know? There was, like, all that drama in school, not like TV vampire drama, but like *interpersonal* drama, which is totally dull and who needs it, you know? Although sometimes I worry I missed out on a real, like, authentic experience, you know?"

Oliver and Celia didn't know. What was he talking about? Was this how actors really talked?

"I am sure you are wondering what this is all about," Professor Rasmali-Greenberg said. And indeed, they were.

"An exciting opportunity has materialized," he told them. "Corey Brandt would like to hire the services of our Explorer-in-Residence"—the professor smiled at Dr. Navel—"and his family, as consultants on his hit show, *The Adventuring Celebrity*."

"*The Celebrity Adventurist*," Celia whispered. Corey Brandt smiled at her. The room seemed to get brighter from the light of his teeth. Celia's knees went weak and she leaned on Oliver for support.

Oliver rolled his eyes. Girls were weird.

"That's right," said Corey. "I have decided to make the new season all about great discoveries, and no one makes greater discoveries than the Navel family." He fist-bumped Oliver for no apparent reason.

"I was just telling young Mr. Brandt how you two are experts on the lost cities of the Inca!" Professor Rasmali-Greenberg said.

"We are?" Oliver asked.

"We are?" Celia asked.

"You are!" the professor said.

Celia couldn't tell if he was joking. His face gave nothing away. Why were real people's faces so hard to understand? On *Love at 30,000 Feet* you could always tell what someone was thinking by looking at a close-up of his face. She wished all people overacted like soap-opera stars. Or that she could stand right up in their faces and study them in close-up, but that would probably make people uncomfortable.

The professor continued, putting his arm around Corey Brandt.

"In fact," he said, "Oliver and Celia have a guide to one of the greatest lost cities in the world in their bag right now!"

"We do?" Oliver asked.

"We do?" Celia asked.

"You do!" the professor said.

Celia was dismayed. How did the professor know about Mr. Rondon and the khipu? Did he know that their mother had been back and had he not told them? Why were people always hiding things from them?

"Of course, the only ones who know how to read it fled into the Amazon rain forest six hundred years ago," the professor told Corey Brandt. "But if anyone could find them, I bet it would be the Navels."

"But—" Oliver was interrupted by a knock at the door.

Dr. Navel looked at his children admiringly as he went to the door. He swung it open to reveal the most wonderful sight the twins had ever seen: the cable guy.

His uniform was bright blue and his tools shined in his tool belt. He looked at the clipboard in his hand.

"I'm looking for Ogden Navel," he said. "I'm from CableWorld. We're here to install your premium package: two hundred and fifty channels in high definition, unlimited video on demand, and a free hat."

Celia yelped and jumped a little off her feet. Oliver smiled. He liked the hat too.

We should observe that in all our lives, there will come days of astounding wonder. Lights shine brighter; food tastes better. Misery is washed away by triumph and all our hopes are realized. These are the days that we each treasure for the entire length of our lives.

For Oliver and Celia, this was *not* one of those days.

"Ah yes," Dr. Navel said. "Unfortunately, we'll have to reschedule. We're traveling soon, you see, and my children were suspended from school. So no cable today. Can you find your way out?"

"Um," the cable guy answered.

"You just go down the stairs, under the polar bear, past the spears, and through the wide double doors beneath the Mesopotamian archway." He closed the door in the cable guy's face.

Oliver and Celia stood in stunned agony.

"Cold," Corey Brandt whispered. He started sending text messages on his cell phone, trying to look busy. Professor Rasmali-Greenberg studied his tie.

"Where were we?" Dr. Navel put his hands together. "Oh yes, the Inca's Itinerary! You had it all along? May I see it? You know, the Incas didn't call it the Amazon River. That name came from the Spanish, after a mythological race of female warriors, Amazonians, and it was only after—"

"This is so unfair!" Celia shouted, interrupting her father and storming off to her room.

"Celia, come back!" Dr. Navel called after her. "Celia, listen, honey, I just wanted you guys to—"

Dr. Navel was interrupted by another knock on the door.

Flustered, he stepped back over to the door and started speaking as he opened it. "I'm sorry, sir, I meant *past* the polar bear and *under* the spears . . ." But the cable guy wasn't there. For a second it looked like no one was at the door. But then a little man cleared his throat and everyone looked down. Sir Edmund stood in the doorway, dressed in a khaki explorers outfit with a pith helmet tucked under his arm. Two servants stood behind him holding large designer duffel bags.

He smoothed his extravagant mustache with his fingers and stepped into the apartment without being invited.

"I couldn't help but hear that your children had been suspended from school. I do hope they are ready to travel again. Per the terms of our wager, I am taking them with me to the Amazon."

16

WE ARE NOT ON VACATION

SIR EDMUND'S SERVANTS followed him into the apartment and set his bags down in the middle of the floor.

"Mr. Brandt, how lovely of you to visit us from Hollywood," he said, although he said "Hollywood" the way you might say "boogers."

"Do I know this guy?" Corey Brandt asked no one in particular.

"Professor, happy to see you," Sir Edmund added, although everyone knew that he was never happy to see anyone. Then he turned to Oliver. "I see you made it back from Machu Picchu in one piece. Where is your sister? Did she have an accident with the llama? She looked a little unsteady on it."

"I'm just fine," Celia said as she burst out of her room and stomped down the hall. "I can ride a llama as well as anyone." She glanced over at Corey Brandt. "Maybe better, actually."

Oliver noticed that she had changed clothes and that her hair was different.

"You didn't come here just to harass my children about llamas," Dr. Navel interrupted.

"Well, I was talking to my old friend Barbara Deaver," said Sir Edmund, "who happens to be a middle school principal. Naturally, I asked after the well-being of my favorite Navels and was saddened to learn they had been suspended from the sixth grade so early." He shook his head. "I fear that too much television has turned them into antisocial deviants. All hope is not lost, however. I can whip them into shape for you, Navel. A few more weeks traveling with me, and they'll be as good as . . ." He twirled his mustache and smiled as he drew out the last word: "Gold."

"The terms of the wager are that they belong to you when they are on *vacation*," Dr. Navel responded. "Suspension is not a vacation."

"Yes it is," Sir Edmund said.

"No it's not," Dr. Navel answered.

"It is," said Sir Edmund.

"It is not," said Dr. Navel.

Oliver, Celia, Corey Brandt, and the professor snapped their heads back and forth between the two men like they were watching a tennis match. Although, given the height difference between Dr. Navel and Sir Edmund, it was more like a tennis match on a steep hill.

"It is."

"It's not."

"It is."

"It's not."

"Enough!" Sir Edmund finally shouted. "I will not stand here and argue with an explorer who cannot even find his own wife." He turned to the professor. "I am amazed you allow him to remain the Explorer-in-Residence. Perhaps the standards of the Explorers Club are slipping. Perhaps I should consider reducing the amount of my next donation . . ."

"There is no need to do that," Professor Rasmali-Greenberg sputtered. "I am sure we can come to an agreement here."

"I thought we might," Sir Edmund said. "Very good then. We shall all travel together to the Amazon."

"No we will not!" Dr. Navel shouted.

"Yes we will," said Sir Edmund.

"We will not!" said Dr. Navel.

"We will indeed!"

"We will absolutely not!"

"We most certainly will!"

"Dude!" Corey Brandt interrupted. "I can't take any more of these bad vibes. Whatever. We'll all go." He turned to Sir Edmund. "Just try to stay off camera, okay?"

"Excellent," said Sir Edmund. "It will be delightful to see television magic in the making. Will your entourage be joining us?"

"I'll be on my own," said Corey Brandt.

"No legal guardians? Assistants? Publicists? Hairstylists? Stuntmen?"

Corey Brandt clenched his jaw and glared at Sir Edmund. "My parents don't travel, my assistant is on vacation, my publicist doesn't *do* nature, this is just how my hair looks, and I"—he coughed into his hand—"I do all my own stunts."

"Really?" Oliver gasped. "So when Agent Zero escaped from the Assassins' Guild in the desert of Kazakhstan, you did that? And jumping out of the sky castle of Mumbai? And waterskiing through the fires of Cleveland? You did all that?"

"Yeah," said Corey Brandt.

"Cool!" said Oliver.

Dr. Navel wondered why Oliver thought it was cool when Corey Brandt did exciting and dangerous things, but awful and dull when Dr. Navel had his children do them.

"I took you to Cleveland once," he muttered to himself.

"I assume we shall start our expedition with Benjamin Constant. I shall make the arrangements," said Sir Edmund. He didn't wait for an answer before he turned to leave. Just before he walked out, he stopped in the doorway.

"One more thing." He turned to Oliver. "My lizard, please."

Oliver looked at Beverly and then looked at Sir Edmund. He thought about how she had saved him from the bat, and shared a snack cake with him, and how she had jumped on Greg Angstura's face. He was about to protest when he remembered she was a lizard. And he didn't like lizards. He went over to the easy chair she had occupied and picked her up.

"Later, Beverly," he said.

She hissed, but Oliver didn't think she meant it

to be mean. Sir Edmund tucked her under his arm and marched out, the servants lugging his bags behind him. He slammed the door as he left.

"Ouch!" they heard him yell as the moon rock fell off its shelf for the second time that day.

Oliver and Celia saw their father smirk.

Across the street, from a high balcony, a woman in black held a telescope and watched through the apartment window. She chewed on a jade toothpick as she read their lips and made out every word the Navels and their guest said. As Sir Edmund stormed out of the apartment, the notorious grave robber Janice McDermott chuckled. Everything was falling into place.

"El Dorado," she said to herself. She wrote the word *gold* in her notebook, followed by three exclamation points.

Revenge was so close she could taste it.

17

WE ARE A LONG WAY FROM HOLLYWOOD

BENJAMIN CONSTANT had never seen anything like this expedition before. They arrived on two single-engine seaplanes. One was for people and one was for the dozens of bags, boxes, trunks, and pieces of equipment that they brought with them. There was a trunk filled with different outfits for Sir Edmund and a trunk filled with Corey Brandt's hair products.

Oliver and Celia had just a backpack that they shared between them. They liked to travel light. Even better would be not to travel at all.

Before you grow concerned that there is yet another disreputable character involving himself in the trials and tribulations of Oliver and Celia Navel, we should observe that Benjamin Constant is not a man but the name of a sleepy logging town on the southern bank of the Amazon River. There have been several men in history called Benjamin Constant, but they are about as well known as the town in the Amazon that bears their name. Visitors rarely arrive and when they do, they do not stay long.

So it came as quite a shock to the residents of Benjamin Constant when two seaplanes buzzed overhead and turned in a tight swirl to land in the river. It came as even more of a shock when a handsome teenager with a handheld video camera and perfect hair leaped from the airplane and swam, fully clothed, to the shore. He climbed out, soaked in the waters of the Amazon River, and squatted on the ground. He pointed the camera at himself and looked dramatically into the lens.

"We have survived a perilous journey through wind and rain, across the great expanse of South America," Corey Brandt told the camera. "We've arrived at this isolated town at the very end of civilization. From the sky, all we could see in any direction was the great Amazon River snaking through the thick green canopy of the rain forest, which has claimed the lives of countless explorers before me. I hope that I, Corey Brandt, will not be its next victim."

A crowd of townspeople gathered. Children hid behind their parents and peered out from between their legs. Fishermen hauled in their nets and stood to watch. Some of the burly loggers laughed and whispered crude comments about the young man.

He furrowed his eyebrows in a look of serious concern and then gave the camera a smirk and a wink. Several village girls would later recall feeling weak in the knees for reasons they could not explain. A few of the burly loggers too. It was a heck of a smile.

"Cut!" Corey Brandt said and dropped the camera back into his pocket. In the meantime, the airplanes had pulled up to the rickety dock just a few feet away and let their engines whine to a stop.

Oliver and Celia, green in the face from the choppy ride in the seaplane, hopped down onto the dock, followed by their father, dressed all in khaki, his smile wide and excited. He waved at the gathered residents of Benjamin Constant.

"*Hola!*" he called.

"Out of the way, Navel," Sir Edmund yelled

from behind him. He started pulling dollar bills from different pockets in his vest and waving them at the townspeople. Then he pointed at his bags in the other plane. Children came running and grabbed the bags for him. "The universal language," he sneered as the children ran off with his bags to the only hotel in town.

"Why'd Corey Brandt dive into the water?" Oliver wondered.

"He knows how to make an entrance," Celia answered dreamily.

"Well, he didn't need to be all wet. And anyway, it'd be cooler if he rode on one of those." Oliver pointed toward a group of rusty old motorcycle taxis. The drivers stood next to their bikes, hoping the foreigners would want a ride. There was not a lot of work for a motorcycle taxi driver in town. They all smiled and nodded when Oliver pointed at them.

Oliver tried to hide his excitement. He could never admit it to his sister, but he kind of wanted to ride on a motorcycle. He kind of wanted Corey Brandt to *see* him ride on a motorcycle. He'd never had the urge do anything dangerous before, but somehow just being around the teen star made him want to be braver.

Celia, on the other hand, did *not* want Corey Brandt to see her try to ride a motorcycle. Being around the teen star made her desperately want to avoid embarrassing herself.

"Greetings! Greetings!" a man in the crowd called out, stepping forward.

He wore a white linen suit and a tie with golden tie clip. He was bald, but sported a tidy beard and mustache. He went immediately over to Corey Brandt. "It is a pleasure to have you here, Mr. Brandt," he said, shaking the teenager's hand. "I am a big fan of *Sunset High*. I do wish you had ended up with Lauren instead of Annabel, but alas . . . great loves are often doomed." He sighed, but it didn't seem to bother Corey Brandt. He was used to it. "We are a long way from Hollywood," the man continued at last, "but I assure you that we will do our best to make you comfortable in our town. I am the mayor of Benjamin Constant, and I am at your service."

He shook hands with their whole group. Oliver and Celia thought they saw a knowing glance pass between Sir Edmund and the mayor. Oliver and Celia knew a thing or two about knowing glances. They exchanged them with each other all the time.

Sometimes the knowing glance meant "Are we really going to watch this?" and sometimes it meant "I can't believe how many commercial breaks there are in this show," and sometimes it meant "On the count of three we are going to jump over this pit of scorpions." But when adults gave each other knowing glances, it always meant trouble for the Navel twins.

Two black Mercedes town cars sliced through the crowd. The mayor gestured to them.

"For you, Mr. Brandt," the mayor said.

Corey Brandt thanked the mayor and went to the first car. The mayor directed Sir Edmund, Dr. Navel, and the twins toward the second car.

"Hey, why don't you take one of those?" Oliver called out, pointing at the motorcycle taxis. The drivers all smiled and revved their engines. "It'd be a much cooler entrance into town. I could film it for you!"

Dr. Navel looked at his son in surprise. Oliver was showing excitement about something that wasn't on television.

Corey Brandt, however, did not look excited about the idea.

"Why don't you two come ride with me?" he suggested. "That'd be even more fun than riding some—" He didn't even have a chance to finish his sentence before Celia was climbing into the black Mercedes.

"But he rides a motorcycle in the opening credits," Oliver said to himself, a little confused. He followed his sister.

"There's a TV in here," Celia exclaimed. The mayor, Sir Edmund, and their father climbed into the second car and they pulled away from the dock as the seaplanes started their engines and took off again, leaving a long wake in the smooth waters of the Amazon.

"So, you're fans of my work?" Corey Brandt asked, pouring them all Diet Cokes from the minibar in the back of the car.

"Yeah," Oliver said as he sipped on the fizzy drink and tried to get the small television to work.

"You too?" Corey asked Celia.

"I . . . um . . ."

"My sister liked you better in *Sunset High* than in *Agent Zero*, but we both like *The Celebrity*

Adventurist," Oliver said. Oliver couldn't believe his sister was letting him do so much of the talking. She was usually the talker. It must have been the shock of sixth grade, or maybe the change in climate in South America.

"I wanted to ask you two—," Corey started to say, but just then Madam Mumu's latest hit single, "Funky Bookmobile," blared through the car.

"I'd show you something new, but your book is overdue . . ."

"Hold on a sec," Corey said, and pulled out his cell phone. "You got Corey!" He even smiled when he answered the phone. "Uh-huh . . . Uh-huh . . . Uh-huh . . . No way! . . . Impossible. I'm in South America right now, with the Navels. Yes, I guarantee we'll talk later. Ciao." He hung up again. "Sorry," he told the twins. "I thought ninth-grade algebra was hard, but just *being* Corey Brandt is a full-time job. Sometimes I wish I could—" His phone rang again.

"I'd show you something new, but your book is overdue . . ."

"You got Corey," he answered it. While he argued with somebody on the other end of the phone,

Oliver watched the muddy town pass by the car windows.

Celia stared at the star. She couldn't believe she was riding in a car with Corey Brandt! In person, he looked older than on TV, probably because he wasn't wearing makeup. She liked seeing him in a way none of the other girls in her class had. She felt special.

"Sorry," Corey said as he hung up the phone again. "I just wanted to tell you two that I really think it's great that you get to have all these adventures. I mean, having Dr. Ogden Navel as your father! You two must have, like, the best time ever. What's your favorite country? India? Tibet?"

"Tibet was full of dangerous—," Oliver started.

"Oh, *snap*!" Corey Brandt shouted. "You've been to Tibet! I'm so jealous! I've always dreamed of going there, but you know, with *Sunset High* and *Agent Zero* and now *The Celebrity Adventurist*, there's just never time. Plus my mom, she'd *never* let me go. Can you believe it? Me? Corey Brandt? I mean, I'm sixteen now, you know? So was Tibet, like, *spiritual*? Was it amazing? Did you meet a lama?"

"Yeah, but he tried to kill—," Oliver started.

"It was great," Celia interrupted him. "It was . . . like . . . *sooo* spiritual."

Oliver gave her a knowing glance of his own, one with raised eyebrows and a questioning look, but she ignored him. Just as she was trying to think of something else to say about Tibet that didn't involve killer witches, murderous lamas, or their mother's secret society, the car arrived at the hotel.

Calling it a hotel, however, was an exaggeration. It looked more like a haunted house. In fact, many of the citizens of Benjamin Constant believed that it was haunted. It had been the mansion of a wealthy rubber baron over a hundred years ago.

Rumor had it that cannibal tribes in the jungle beyond the town didn't like him taking the rubber from their trees, so they broke into the house and ate him and his entire family. It was said that late at night you could hear the ghosts of the rubber baron and his family groaning, doomed forever to live in the house where they had been turned into a feast for cannibals.

That story didn't bother Oliver and Celia,

though. As they pulled up to the mansion, they looked right up to the roof and saw the most glorious sight: a shining round satellite dish pointed at the sky. Oliver was out of the car before it had even stopped.

"Excuse me." Celia smiled an apology at Corey Brandt, snatched up her backpack, and ran off after her brother. If he got to the television first, she'd never get to pick what she wanted to watch.

18

WE OOO-LA-LA AND BLAH-BLAH-BLAH

OLIVER AND CELIA ran right through the foyer of the crumbling mansion, which now served as the lobby, and bounded up the grand winding staircase, with its frayed red carpeting, to the suite at the top of the stairs.

"The suite is for Mr. Brandt!" the manager called after them, but Oliver and Celia weren't listening. They burst through the doors and raced for the table next to the couch where the remote control was resting. Oliver was ahead, with Celia, who was much faster up the stairs, chasing close behind. She saw that Oliver would make it first, so she dove and tackled him around the ankles.

"Ow!" he shouted as he crashed to the floor.

Celia sprang over him and grabbed the remote in a dive roll, landing on her behind with the device pointed straight at the TV.

"Ha!" she said, preparing to turn the TV on, when it snapped on, apparently by itself. "What the—"

"Universal remote," Oliver smirked, waving their remote control from home in the air. In his other hand he held the hollowed-out book. He'd carried the remote to South America in secret. The universal remote would work on any television in the world. Celia wondered why she hadn't thought of that.

Oliver tuned the TV to the Game Show Network. *Name That Vegetable* was on. Celia used her remote to switch it to the Décor Channel to watch *House Heroes*. Oliver changed it to Cartoon Classics One. Celia changed it back to *House Heroes*. Oliver changed it to the Cooking Channel. Celia put it back to *House Heroes*.

"I want to watch *House Heroes*. They're giving a family a new house after their last one blew up."

"That's the boringest show in the world,"

Oliver complained. He changed it back to *Name That Vegetable*.

"Is not." Celia flipped it back. A computer graphic showed someone dropping a Velma Sue's snack cake into a bathtub, causing a disastrous flood.

Oliver changed it to cartoons. Celia changed it back. Flood, cartoons, flood, cartoons, flood.

"This is never going to work," Celia said. "If we're going to watch anything, we'll have to cooperate."

"Sure," Oliver said. "You say that now. You didn't want to cooperate when you tackled me."

"Well, things have changed."

"They sure have. Why are you so weird around Corey Brandt?"

"I'm not weird," Celia snapped. "You're weird." She did her best impression of Oliver. *"Hey, Corey, I think you're so great in whatever and can you tell me about thingamajig and I just loved you in blah-blah-blah . . ."*

"You can't blah-blah-blah *Agent Zero*!"

"I can blah-blah-blah whatever I want."

"Well at least I didn't get all gushy and mushy and ooo-la-la-y."

"I did *not* get all gushy and mushy and ooo-la-la-y."

"Oh, Corey!" Oliver danced around, doing his impression of Celia in a singsong falsetto. *"Tibet was like . . . sooo spiritual! Nobody tried to kill us or get us to find the Lost Library or make us fight a yeti. We should go there. . . . We could fall into a pit together . . . a deep spiritual pit!"*

"Hey Corey, hey Corey, hey Corey!" Celia stood up to jump around like an eager puppy, which is how she thought Oliver was acting. *"Hey Corey, pay attention to me! I think you're the coolest. Will you be my friend? Will you do a backflip? Wanna ride motorcycles? Wanna play dodgeball? Hey Corey, hey Corey, hey Corey!"*

"I was not like that."

"Yes you were."

"Was not."

"Was too."

"Was not."

"Was too."

"I don't think either of you were like that," said Corey Brandt, leaning on the door frame with his arms crossed like an ad in a magazine. An ad for cool.

Both children turned as red as boiled beets.

"You . . . were . . . standing . . . there . . . ?" Celia gasped. "The . . . whole . . . time?"

"Don't worry about it," Corey said, strolling into the room. "You wouldn't believe how crazy people get around me sometimes, just because I'm, like, superfamous. But that's just TV. I'm a totally normal guy. I actually wanted to ask you something before we go into the jungle. I wonder if I could see the—"

"I'd show you something new, but your book is overdue . . ." The words to "Funky Bookmobile" blasted through the room.

"Hold on a sec," Corey said as he pulled out his cell phone. "You got Corey." He stepped back out into the hall. "I told you not to call me here . . ."

Just then, Dr. Navel and Sir Edmund came into the room arguing.

"We cannot simply enter the Javari Valley without proper permits!" Dr. Navel shouted. "There are uncontacted tribes living there. They have never seen an outsider before. They have a right to their privacy!"

"Nonsense!" Sir Edmund shouted.

"We'll get them to sign privacy-release forms," Corey Brandt called from the hallway.

Sir Edmund rolled his eyes.

"I have a duty as a scientist," Dr. Navel said. "I must respect those cultures who choose not to contact the outside world. I know it means nothing to you, but true explorers have a code of ethics."

"Oh, you can stuff your ethics!" Sir Edmund retorted. "Cannibals don't care about your ethics. One shot from their poison darts and your ethics won't mean a thing."

"We do not know that they are cannibals," Dr. Navel said.

"Cannibals?" Oliver gulped, looking sideways at Celia.

"Why don't you go to the museum and do some research then?" Sir Edmund mocked Dr. Navel. "Go look into your stuffy books. The rest of us will go into the jungle and make TV magic."

"Since when do you care about TV magic?" said Dr. Navel.

"I have always loved TV magic! Isn't that true, children? I watched the television with you all summer, did I not?"

Just as Oliver and Celia were not very good at adventuring, Sir Edmund was not very good at watching television. During their time with him, they had stayed in the fanciest hotels, which had a lot of TV channels. Even so, Celia made them watch reruns of *Love at 30,000 Feet*.

Sir Edmund was always asking who people were and why they were doing whatever they were doing. He forgot the answers almost as soon as Celia told him. He couldn't tell Captain Sinclair and Copilot Rogerson apart, and every time the Duchess in Business Class fainted, Sir Edmund would tell a story about a real duchess in Norway who was narcoleptic. Then he would explain that narcoleptics were people with a condition that caused them to fall asleep with no warning all the time. By the time he finished his story, they'd have missed half the episode and something else would be coming on.

In answer to his question, Oliver and Celia shrugged.

"See?" Sir Edmund said.

"They shrugged," Dr. Navel said. "That means no."

"When a child shrugs, it means yes."

"I think I know my children better than you. A shrug means no."

"It means yes."

"It means no."

"Yes."

"No."

They continued arguing like that as they passed through the sitting room into the bedroom of Corey Brandt's suite and closed the door. They didn't ask Oliver and Celia to say what they actually meant by shrugging, which was a relief.

"This is going to be a long trip," said Oliver.

"Yeah," Celia agreed.

"Sir Edmund doesn't care about *The Celebrity Adventurist* or TV magic, no matter what he was saying."

"He wants the guide to El Dorado. That's what he was looking for in Machu Picchu."

"The key-poop."

"You know it's called a khipu."

"I like my way better."

"Well, whatever it is, it's not safe for us to have it. Principal Deaver was wearing the symbol of the Council. She probably told Sir Edmund that we had it. I bet that's why she suspended us . . . so we would go down here and find people to translate it."

"And once we do," said Oliver, "Sir Edmund will go on his own to El Dorado. He probably plans to leave us in the jungle."

"Why do you think he wants to find El Dorado so badly? Because of the gold?"

Celia wondered if Oliver remembered what their mother told them in Tibet. She had said that the Lost Library of Alexandria would be found in a lost place—a blank spot on the map. What could be more blank than El Dorado? Most people didn't even believe it existed. She also remembered the prophecy they'd been told: *All that is known will be unknown and what was lost will be found.* Could this all be part of their destiny? Getting suspended from school, going to the Amazon, and even Corey Brandt?

"Sorry, guys." Corey Brandt came back into the room. "Hollywood can be so tough, you know? It's like everybody wants something from you and you never know who you can trust. That's why I wanted to come to the Amazon. Exploring just seems so much more, like, honest, you know?"

Celia gave Oliver a knowing glance that said,

"Don't tell him anything about the khipu or the Mnemones or the Council or our prophecy."

Oliver nodded. He understood.

"So what are we doing?" Corey Brandt smiled. "Watching the History Channel?"

Oliver and Celia looked over at the TV and saw a key with ancient Greek writing below it covering the screen. A little cartoon man in a toga was tapping his foot in the corner. Somehow, in wrestling over the remote, they'd accessed the Catalog of the Lost Library—and Corey Brandt was looking right at it.

The image suddenly changed to a very old map of the world where none of the continents were in the right place. In the middle was a large island that looked like it was pushing the rest of the land out of the way. There was some writing on the drawing that the twins recognized as ancient Greek, even though they couldn't read what it said. The island was labeled only with a picture—a scroll wrapped in chains.

"Hey," said Corey Brandt. "I've seen that before. Isn't that the symbol that Sir Edmu—"

He was interrupted by a loud crash and the sound of breaking glass. Screams came through the door to the bedroom, followed by bangs as furniture crashed to the floor.

"We mean you no harm!" they heard their father shout.

"Savages!" they heard Sir Edmund shout.

Then they heard a loud thump, like a body hitting the floor, and then a quieter thump, like a smaller body hitting the floor.

They all ran to the bedroom and burst through the door. They saw a scene of absolute chaos. Furniture was overturned. The windows were shattered. Sir Edmund and their father were gone.

"What happened to my hotel room?" cried Corey Brandt. "And where did those two go?"

Celia reached up to the door frame and plucked a long dart from the wood. Its needle-thin point glistened with poison.

"Cannibals," said Celia. "I think cannibals just kidnapped our father."

19

WE UPSET SOME CHICKENS

OLIVER RAN to the smashed window and looked out over the jungle. He saw nothing but thick green foliage and dark shadows. He craned his neck around to look toward the river in the distance.

"What do you see?" Celia asked.

"I thought I saw . . . I don't know. . . . Wait! There!" He pointed. Celia rushed over and saw a large man running with their father slung over his shoulder and a smaller one carrying Sir Edmund. The figures were painted in black and red, so it was impossible to make out their identity, but they were nearly at the river already.

"That one with Sir Edmund looks like a woman," Oliver said.

"Amazonians . . . ," whispered Corey Brandt.

"We have to follow them!" Celia shouted, and turned from the window ledge.

"We can't go running after cannibals into the Amazon!" said Corey Brandt.

"We don't even know if they are cannibals," said Oliver.

"They were half naked, covered in body paint, and shooting poison darts," said Celia. "Does it really matter what cuisine they prefer? They took Dad! We have to go after them!"

"Corey's kind of right, though," Oliver said. "We can't go *running* after them."

Celia exhaled angrily. Why was her brother so difficult?

"But we can go *driving . . . ,*" Oliver said. "On motorcycles!"

The motorcycle taxi drivers were sitting around outside the hotel playing dominoes and hoping that the first tourists they'd had in ages would need to go somewhere, like the local tavern. Or the other local tavern. Or the third local tavern. Pretty much all there was to do at night in Benjamin Constant was go to the taverns.

When Oliver and Celia ran out of the front doors of the hotel calling for taxis, the drivers were a little surprised that children so young would want to go the taverns. It made much more sense when the children panted, "The river . . . as fast as you can."

The teenager with the perfect hair followed behind.

"I . . . um . . . ," Corey called out as Oliver and Celia each mounted a motorcycle behind the driver. "I don't know how to ride one of those things!"

"But you ride one in the opening credits!" Oliver called back over the thundering engines revving up.

"I mean, right . . ." Corey Brandt kicked his toe at the dirt. "I meant this type of motorcycle . . . I've never ridden this *type*."

Oliver looked over at his sister, who shrugged. Oliver couldn't believe Corey Brandt didn't know how to ride a motorcycle. He was Agent Zero! He was the Celebrity Adventurist! He was a teenager!

"Just get on and hold on tight," Oliver said. "The driver will do the driving!"

Corey nodded and hopped on, pulling his camera from his pocket to film the chase. They screeched off, one by one, toward the river, kicking up a cloud of dust as they went. Wild dogs barked as they zoomed past.

Celia felt like every bone in her body was being rattled into dust by the bumps and jostles of the motorcycle. The backpack on her back caught the air as they drove and it felt like she was being yanked off the seat. This was not a pleasant feeling.

Oliver couldn't wipe the smile off of his face. They hit an incline and took to the air.

"Woo-hoo!" he yelled as the bike flew. Then it came down with a hard thump that smashed his mouth shut with a snap and bounced him off the seat. "Ow-ahh!" he yelled and caught onto the driver's jacket just before he was hurled off the motorcycle. He squeezed tightly. Maybe motorcycles weren't all that much fun after all. He hoped that Corey hadn't been recording him.

They sped through the town. Women hanging the wash out to dry shouted as they splashed through puddles, spraying mud onto freshly cleaned sheets. Old men dozing in hammocks yelled at them to quiet down. Little children scattered screaming in front of them, and chickens

clucked angrily to the side of road. The Navels were not making any friends in Benjamin Constant. It felt just like Mr. McNulty's class.

They came to a skidding halt, one after the other, at the riverbank. Oliver leaped off the bike and stared down. He couldn't see where the kidnappers had gone.

"What do we do now? They got away!" said Oliver.

"We have to go after them!" said Celia. "We don't have cable yet! And we can't let Dad get eaten!"

"We don't know that they are cannibals!"

"I fear, indeed, that they are cannibals," a smooth voice from behind them said. The mayor stood by his idling Mercedes, puffing on a thin cigar. He looked at the long dart that Celia still clutched in her hand. "That is the weapon of the *Cozinheiros*. At least, that is what we call them. It means 'the cooks.' We do not know what they call themselves, as no one has ever met them and survived to ask."

"Why do you call them the cooks?" Oliver gulped.

The mayor just tilted his head and nodded knowingly at Oliver.

"Oh," he said. "'The cooks' sounds a little nicer than 'the cannibals.'"

An angry crowd was beginning to gather behind the mayor. They were upset about their sheets and their naps and their games and their chickens. People did not go racing and shouting through Benjamin Constant. It was frowned upon.

"Can we call the police?" Celia asked. "Or the army or something? You're the mayor!"

"Sadly, this tribe comes from the Javari Valley. My authority does not extend into that region. It is a land of protected tribes who neither have nor want contact with the outside world. We cannot trespass on their land."

He nodded gravely, but some of the loggers behind him chuckled. Celia wondered why. There was nothing funny about a tribe of cooks kidnapping their father.

"So what should we do?" Oliver demanded. He was sick of all these adults who put them in danger and offered no help to get them out. It just wasn't fair.

"Well," the mayor thought out loud. "You have little time. From what we know of these tribes, they will not keep prisoners for long. Your only chance will be to locate their village and perhaps negotiate for the release of your father and Sir Edmund."

"How do we do that?"

The mayor shrugged. "I cannot grant you permission to enter the valley. I can, I suppose, look the other way if you go on your own. But there will be no help for you from the authorities."

"How are we supposed to find them in all that jungle?"

The mayor chuckled. "There are no secrets in the rain forest. You will be seen from the moment you enter their territory. All you must do is get there."

"Where is their territory?" asked Celia.

"There is a bend where the river twists like an ampersand," the mayor answered. "A small tributary breaks off from the main branch at this point."

"What's an ampersand?" Oliver asked.

"That weird 'and' symbol," Celia said.

"And what's a tributary?"

"It's a smaller river," said Celia.

"*Wally Worm's Word World*?" the mayor asked. Celia nodded.

"There's a twist in the river," the mayor continued. "A smaller river breaks off of it. If you follow that smaller river, you will arrive in the Javari Valley. I am certain that your enemies will come to you. It will only be a matter of finding the right ones."

"The right ones?" Oliver wondered.

"There are many unknown tribes in the valley. You will be seen as a trespasser by all of them."

"Great," said Celia. "Just great."

"How are we supposed to even get there?" Oliver asked. "We don't have a boat."

"Take mine!" a man shouted from the crowd.

"Or mine!" another shouted.

"Take my husband's," a woman called out.

Soon half the town had offered their boats to the Navel twins.

"Generous people," said Corey Brandt.

"They just want to get rid of us," said Celia.

"Well, it worked," Oliver said. "Let's go before they get too far away with Dad."

"Why are you so adventurous all of a sudden?" Celia asked her brother as they climbed onto a small canoe with an outboard motor.

"No reason." Oliver shrugged, glancing at Corey Brandt, who was starting up the motor.

"Oh," said Celia. "I get it."

Celia could understand Oliver trying to impress the TV star; she just wished they could do it from the safety of their hotel room. They had rescued their father before, as much as it annoyed them, but she worried that this time they'd all become dinner for cannibals in the process.

But she wasn't about to say anything. She didn't want Corey Brandt to think she was a wuss. She was way tougher than Oliver.

She just prayed she wouldn't have to prove it in the jungle.

20

WE DO NOT HEAR PEACE DRUMS

THE SUN SANK below the horizon as they sped away from town. Darkness swept over them. Soon they could see nothing on either side of the river but the trees nearest the bank. Beyond them, all was black. Corey steered the boat and kept his camera propped between his knees so he could film himself. Celia and Oliver held flashlights they'd found and scanned the river for signs of . . . well, anything. Bugs swarmed in the beams of light.

They couldn't hear each other over the roar of the motor, so they rode without talking. Celia thought about losing their father and becoming orphans. Oliver wondered if, somehow, their mother might show up to save them. She'd done it in Tibet. He really hoped she'd do it again. They could really use some saving.

Celia flicked her flashlight on and saw a big log up ahead, almost the same length as their boat. They were about to crash into it. Just as she was about to signal Corey to turn, her light caught a red gleam on the log, like a jewel.

"What the—?" she began to wonder, when the red gleam blinked and the whole log dove under the surface. "Alligator!" she yelled.

"What?" Oliver yelled back.

"I saw an alligator!"

"No you didn't!"

"Yes I did!"

"No you didn't! You saw a black caiman! They're related to the alligator, but they are native to the Amazon River." He smiled at Celia. "Nature Channel. Reptile Reruns Week."

Celia rolled her eyes. She didn't like the Nature Channel. And she really didn't like Oliver knowing more than she did.

They sped onward for hours. Celia wondered why they hadn't caught up with the Cozinheiros yet. Something wasn't right. Their motorboat had to be faster than a canoe. She looked back at Corey Brandt, who was focused on driving the boat and not crashing into anything in the dark. She couldn't believe that the teen star was really there and that he was helping them save their father. She wondered if he'd be upset that the kidnapping had messed up his expedition. She would apologize later. And maybe she'd ask him why he chose Annabel over Lauren at the end of *Sunset High*. She'd heard a rumor that it was because he was dating Annabel in real life.

Celia dozed off, thinking about *Sunset High* and celebrity gossip. Oliver too fell sound asleep. As they slept, Corey Brandt pulled out his cell phone and made a call.

"I'm going in," he said. "There's been a problem."

Oliver and Celia woke to the screech of birds hunting for breakfast. A pod of pink river dolphins played in the wake of their boat, leaping from side to side in a playful race. The sun had risen and they were approaching the tight twist in the river that the mayor had told them about.

Corey turned the boat slowly onto the narrow tributary, and the dolphins did not follow. The trees hung over the banks, leaning in on each other from both sides to form an archway. The river looked like a long emerald corridor in the palace of a lunatic king. Mist rose off the water.

The thick canopy of trees blocked out most of the light, so everything was shaded in a green twilight, with streaks of sunlight breaking through to sparkle on the river. The banks narrowed as they urged the boat forward. After a few minutes, they felt like they were in an entirely different world. Corey slowed the motor so they could hear around them.

The silence was shocking. An occasional insect buzzed. A tree rustled. Otherwise, there was nothing. It was as quiet as a school hallway on a Sunday, and just as creepy.

They listened carefully as they moved forward, deeper into the mysterious world of the Javari River valley. They scanned the thick foliage on the banks for any signs of life.

An ink-black jaguar eyed them lazily from a high branch. In this remote part of the world, the animals did not yet know to fear humans. They all kept their eyes fixed on the cat as they passed, but it didn't move.

Celia watched the shadowy forest. She couldn't decide if she was more worried about a wild animal attack or a blowgun attack. Oliver was pretty sure he was equally afraid of both. Corey steered with his mouth hanging open in awe. He kept swatting mosquitoes from his face.

"This is the most beautiful thing I've ever—," he began, but a loud noise interrupted him, shattering the silence.

"I'd show you something new, but your book is overdue . . ." Madam Mumu blared. *"I'd show you something new, but your book is overdue . . ."*

Corey's phone kept ringing.

"Sorry . . . sorry." He fumbled for it. "Amazing we get cell service out here! You got Corey," he answered it. "Oh, it's you. How many times do I have to tell you that I'm in the Amazon? Well, I can't help you. . . . You'll just have to do it yourself. You're the professional, after all." He hung up and stared at his phone a moment, shaking his head. He put it back in his pocket. "Sorry about that. Personal shoppers . . . can't do anything for themselves. Sometimes I wonder if it's worth hiring them, you know?"

Oliver and Celia just stared at him blankly.

They would have continued sitting in awkward silence, but just then they heard a sound up ahead. The beating of drums. The beat was steady and loud and growing faster.

"War drums?" whispered Corey Brandt.

"I don't think there's such a thing as peace drums," said Oliver.

"Shut the engine off!" said Celia.

"Shh!" said Oliver. They ducked low in the boat and listened.

Boom, boom, boom.

The sound came from in front of them.

Boom, boom, boom.

This time it came from behind. In the bush they saw nothing, but the beat continued.

Boom, boom, boom, called the drums ahead of them.

Boom, boom, boom, answered the drums behind.

"Come closer, come closer, come closer." The beat ahead seemed to call out a language older than speaking.

"Come closer and we'll eat you," called the drums from behind.

Boom, boom, boom, boom. Boom, boom, boom.

The water was moving faster and starting to churn with white rapids where the river narrowed over jagged rocks. White foam splashed and sprayed in all directions. Water splashed into the boat. The drums from behind were closing in and the drums from the front were getting closer. The river pushed them forward.

And then they jerked to a sudden stop.

21

WE MAKE A SPLASH

THEY WERE STUCK. The boat had wedged it-self into a large rock in the middle of the river.

"This is not a good place to be stuck," said Oliver, listening to the drums and looking at the rapids ahead of them.

Corey tried to push the boat free with a paddle. It rocked and swayed but didn't move. He tried to start the engine again. He pulled the cord, but nothing happened.

"Uncool," he said.

"We've got to go," said Oliver.

"We're gonna have to swim," said Corey.

"We can't swim," said Celia. "Caiman." She pointed at a group of the black alligator look-alikes that were now circling their boat. "Try the engine again."

She got up to help just as Corey yanked the cord back hard. She got a face full of the teen star's knuckles, which knocked her backward on the boat, right at Oliver.

"Watch out!" Oliver called, but too late. She stepped onto the flashlight he'd set down on the floor. Her foot flew into the air and she went backward off the front of the boat, right past her brother, splashing into the river. It would have been a funny fall if it wasn't about to turn deadly.

"Grab my hand!" Corey shouted, reaching over the edge to rescue Celia.

"Don't lean so far out!" Oliver warned. "I don't weigh enough! You'll tip the—" But it was too late. Corey leaned out and the boat tipped up on its side, dumping them both sideways toward the water.

"Crud," Corey said as they rolled out of the boat and into the river. He actually used a different word than *crud*, but our story is about to get bad enough without adding foul language to its troubles.

Oliver tried to hold on to the boat, which turned sideways and slid right off the rock upside down.

The caiman disappeared below the surface to get out of the way. Oliver was being dragged down the river with the boat.

"Let it go!" shouted Celia.

"But your pack's in there . . . with the remote control . . . and the . . . poop thingy!"

"You know it's called a khipu!" Celia shouted.

"I like my way bet—" Oliver couldn't finish his sentence. Something sucked him underneath the water.

"Oliver!" Celia shouted.

He kicked with all his might for the air and broke the surface with a gasp.

"Just the current!" he said.

"Swim toward the shore!" Celia commanded.

The three of them started to swim as hard as they could toward the riverbank, but the current was much stronger than they were. They were getting pulled into the rapids ahead of them and there wasn't anything they could do about it.

Oliver stopped swimming.

"What . . . are you . . . doing?" Celia panted, still fighting her way toward land.

"It's like a waterslide. We've just gotta ride it to the bottom!" Oliver answered.

"You . . . hate . . . waterslides," she said.

"I hate a lot of things," Oliver replied. "But I'm stuck with most of them!" He let himself be sucked along with the current. It was a heck of a lot easier than fighting a river. Celia lost sight of him in the roiling rapids.

"Oliv—," she called out, only to get a mouthful of water as she was sucked under herself.

Celia had seen music videos where sweaty teenagers slam into each other over and over again, twisting and turning and knocking around from side to side, while a guitar screeches and drums rumble. A mosh pit, it is called, and it is a special feature of heavy-metal culture, long studied by anthropologists, but rarely experienced by eleven-year-old girls. But at this moment, Celia felt like she was in a mosh pit at the bottom of a river.

Her body slammed into the muddy riverbed and then the current tossed her up into a boulder. Then she was pushed aside and spun around and found herself gasping for air at the surface. Just as she caught her breath, she was pulled back under and thrust forward through a narrow channel of rocks, scraping her elbows and she passed. A sneaker whacked her in the head. She got angry that Oliver was kicking her until she realized it was her own sneaker, torn off her foot by the current. She reached out and grabbed it and found herself breaking the surface of the water again.

"Oliver!" she gasped.

"Celia!" Oliver called. She saw her brother a few feet from her, trying to swim toward land again. Corey Brandt was standing on the side of the river, soaked.

"Swim!" he called out.

Celia started to follow her brother. She let her head turn to the side to see why Oliver was swimming so hard and Corey Brandt was shouting. They were fast approaching a waterfall.

"Oh crud," Celia said, except she didn't say *crud* either. Then she and Oliver went right over the edge of the waterfall.

They tumbled head over heels through the air. Sheets of whitewater poured down on top of them as they kicked madly to the surface. They popped up in the calm brown waters of the pool at the bottom of the waterfall.

That wasn't so bad, thought Oliver. Not nearly as bad as the giant waterfall they'd gone over in Tibet. Then he saw the splinters of wood that used to be their boat and realized that he had missed being smashed onto the rocks by only a few inches. Celia was treading water nearby. He was relieved she was safe, though she had a bloody scrape on her forehead.

"We gotta get out of the water fast," Oliver told her.

"Caiman?" Celia gulped, suddenly picturing herself as dinner for an alligator-looking creature.

"No," Oliver said. "But the Amazon is where piranhas live. Everyone knows that!"

Celia shot like a dart to the edge of the pool and practically leaped out of the water. Oliver followed close behind. Just as he was at the water's edge, he saw their backpack snagged on a rock.

"I know what you're thinking, Oliver," Celia said. "Don't do it."

But it was too late. Oliver swam through the water and grabbed the backpack off the rocks and then made his way, exhausted, toward shore.

"Ahh!" he shouted, and disappeared below the surface, just a few feet from Celia.

"Oliver!" she screamed.

"It's okay." Oliver gasped, reappearing. "A twig brushed my leg. I thought it was a piranha." He pulled himself out of the water and flopped onto the riverbank. Celia tied her shoe back on quickly.

"Listen," she said.

"No more drums," said Oliver.

The brush rustled and Oliver and Celia turned and grabbed on to each other. Corey Brandt came stumbling down toward them.

"I think we're safe!" he called out.

"Shhhhh!" Oliver snapped at him.

The three of them crouched in silence on the riverbank for a while to make sure that the drums were gone.

"Well," Celia whispered. "Now what?"

"I have an idea," Corey answered with a smile. He pulled the phone out of his pocket and hit some buttons on it. His smile vanished. "My phone's busted! That was a nice phone!"

"So I guess we're walking," said Celia.

"Yeah." Corey Brandt ran his fingers through his hair. It was somehow perfect again. "Now it's just Corey Brandt versus the wilderness! A real *adventurist*! At least the camera's waterproof."

He dropped the phone back in his pocket and pulled the camera out. He pointed it at himself and hit record. He wrinkled his brow. He smoothed his hair. He pursed his lips. He unpursed them. He pursed them again. Celia was surprised at the amount of lip work that acting demanded. Satisfied with the degree of lip pursing he had achieved, Corey spoke.

"Having barely survived the uncharted rapids, my crew and I were forced to make our way by land into hostile territory. Will we find the dreaded Cozinheiros—cannibals lurking in the forest? Will they find us first? What has become of our companions? I feel a great responsibility, greater than anything I've felt in all my sixteen years." He gazed up into the trees, looking serious and thoughtful. He snapped the camera off.

"Cool, huh? I'm gonna get some cutaway shots of the waterfall and the rapids while you guys rest." He jumped around, filming everything and practicing his dramatic voice, which was deeper and louder than his normal voice.

"I think Corey might be insane," Oliver whispered to his sister.

"It's Hollywood," she replied. "That's how celebrities are." In truth, Celia was worried. She couldn't place it, but something seemed wrong about the teen star. She didn't want to make Oliver nervous, though. "We'll just have to look out for him," she added.

"Sure," said Oliver. "But who's going to look out for us?"

Someone was indeed looking out for them—or rather looking out *at* them. There were a dozen pairs of eyes watching Oliver and Celia from the darkness of the forest, their skillful camouflage rendering them invisible to all but the most careful observer. Their drums were silent. We cannot yet be sure what they intend for our intrepid twins, but we must hope they do not plan to invite our heroes for dinner.

22

WE ADMIRE THE FURNITURE

AS A SCIENTIST, Dr. Ogden Navel could not help but be curious about the nature of the poison that had been shot into him with a dart. As an explorer, he was deeply curious about the painted warriors who had broken into the hotel room and abducted him. But as Oliver and Celia's father, he was terrified. He didn't know what had become of his children, where he was, or why he had been kidnapped.

His head ached, but otherwise he felt fine. He wiggled his fingers. He wiggled his toes. Everything seemed to be working. He also noticed, much to his surprise, that he was not tied up. Nor was he blindfolded. And he was sitting in what appeared to be a plaid armchair in a bland suburban living room.

In his study of the ethnosphere—which is what

an explorer like Dr. Navel would call all the wonderful things that people and cultures have dreamed up since the dawn of civilization, from the Songlines of Australia's Yolngu people to televised celebrity impersonator competitions—Dr. Navel had seen many strange things. He had seen Tendai monks run for a thousand days without breaking a sweat; he had seen a child in Indonesia dance with a black mamba snake; he had seen a sixth-grade classroom. But he had never seen a tribe that kidnapped people and then left them sitting in a plaid armchair. And yet there he was.

The room looked just like the living room he'd grown up in. There was a sofa and a side table. There was a low bookshelf and cabinet for a radio or a television, although it was empty. There was a potted plant. There were two bright windows, the sun slicing through them. The wallpaper was striped, but peeling. The carpeting was brown and moldy, and as his head cleared, Dr. Navel noticed that the room smelled terrible. He saw his glasses sitting on the side table next to him and he slid them on.

As soon as he could see clearly, he noticed that the wallpaper was not striped. Vines were growing up the walls. The potted plant was not a decorative feature of the room, but rather a small tree that had broken through the floor and was growing inside the house.

A gray howler monkey with a shock of black hair on its head perched on the windowsill, watching him carefully. When Dr. Navel stood, the monkey screeched and ran off. Dr. Navel walked out of the living room to look around. He was in a hallway. Discolored paint showed where pictures had once hung on the walls.

"Hello?" he called. *"Hola? Guten Tag?"* He received no response.

Dr. Navel had learned, through a life of travel and awkward dinner conversations, that it was always helpful to know how to say hello in a variety of languages. It was also helpful to know how to say, "Your mother-in-law looks lovely in that dress," but he didn't think that would be helpful at the moment. He might save it for when he met his captors.

"Moino?" he tried, in the Apalai language. *"Pitsupai?"* he tried in a Xingu dialect. Again, he was met with silence.

He wandered down the hallway to an empty

study where the bookshelves had long ago collapsed and rotted, then to a decaying kitchen, where he saw a tree sprouting from a very old refrigerator. The house had clearly been abandoned for a long time.

He found a bedroom at the back of the house. It contained only a rusty metal bed frame, an old steamer trunk, and curtains that had perhaps once been the color of ripe peaches but had been sun baked for so long they looked like the color of overcooked carrots. He opened the trunk. It was filled with Velma Sue's snack cakes, still wrapped in shining plastic and gleaming in unnatural yellows and pinks. He shut the trunk and peered out the window.

He was in the jungle; that much was clear. But this was unlike any jungle he had ever seen. There was a wide street with an overgrown sidewalk, and quaint houses were lined up on both sides of it. Some had collapsed roofs and some of their doors had fallen off their hinges. In the distance, poking over the treetops, he saw a rusty water tower. It was as if someone had taken a nice American suburb and dropped it into the jungle, leaving it to rot. Who would do such a thing?

Bang! Grrr. Bang!

A sudden noise startled him. The noise had come from inside the house, inside this very bedroom.

Bang, bang, bang!

The noise was coming from the closet.

What sort of wild animal could that be? he wondered. A warthog? A panther?

Dr. Navel felt bad for whatever animal was trapped in there. If he were a wild animal, he would be terrified to be stuck in a closet in a suburban housing development.

He reached for the door handle and braced himself. Whatever came out might attack him out of fear, but Dr. Navel never let fear—a jungle creature's or his own—get in the way of curiosity. He could never understand why his children *always* did.

He pulled the door open and leaped to the side to let whatever was in there escape, but nothing ran out. He peered inside and saw what had been making all that noise.

Sir Edmund was curled in a ball in the closet, with his hands and feet tied together and a gag tied in his mouth. He looked up at Dr. Navel in a desperate rage. Dr. Navel bent down and removed the gag.

"Who put you in here?" Dr. Navel demanded. "Where are Oliver and Celia?"

"How should I know? Our captors shot me with a poison dart right after they shot you." Sir Edmund squirmed. "Will you untie me, Navel? I won't lie here talking to you like a trussed pig."

"First you'll answer my questions. I know you won't help me once you're free."

Sir Edmund grunted angrily, but didn't disagree. "My nose itches," he said.

"Did you see anything before you were knocked out?"

"Our captors wore red and black paint on their bodies. I have heard of a tribe of cannibals that paint themselves like that and attack logging camps. It costs a fortune to replace the workers."

"Well, maybe logging companies shouldn't be destroying their forest. You do know that it is a sacred land to the people who live in it."

"Are you really defending them, Navel? For all you know, they might have eaten your children."

"My children, I am sure, can defend themselves. They have survived worse than cannibals. They have survived you, after all."

"I never put your children in more danger than you yourself have, so don't start with that. Exploration isn't a game for children, especially children as dull as yours."

"I will not stand here and have you insult Oliver and Celia. They are brilliant in their own way."

"Brilliant! Ha! My lizard has more smarts than those two brats combined."

Dr. Navel started to close the closet door on him again.

"Wait!" Sir Edmund called out. "We've both been betrayed. Powerful forces are trying to stop us. Ancient forces. They are manipulating your children, putting them in grave danger."

"How do you know that?"

"I *am* one of those forces," he said. "But I am not the only one. If you untie me, I can explain myself."

"I'll untie you after you explain yourself."

"Untie me now, and then I'll explain myself."

"Explain yourself first."

"Untie me first!"

"Explain!"

"Untie me!"

"You are . . . incorrigible!" Dr. Navel threw his hands in the air in frustration. Arguing with this scheming millionaire was like arguing with Oliver and Celia. Especially Celia. And like when he argued with Celia, he never really won. So he bent down to untie the little man. He had to know what Sir Edmund was talking about. He had to save his children from whatever terrible fate lay in store. It was his fault, as usual, that they were in danger.

As he reached for the rope at Sir Edmund's wrists, a voice spoke behind him.

"Are you sure you want to do that?"

He turned quickly to face his captor, who was standing in the doorway, silhouetted by the sunlight.

"The children will be here shortly," she said.

"Oh," said Dr. Navel. And he passed out where he stood.

"I should have known," sneered Sir Edmund as the closet door was slammed shut on him once more.

23

WE ALWAYS WEAR UNDERWEAR

FOR THOSE OF YOU who have never gotten lost in the Amazon rain forest, you should know a few things.

First, it is boring. One thick patch of green looks like the next, on and on for thousands of miles. It is very easy to become lost. It is even easier to become bored.

Second, it is also dark. The darkness is not like night, but like an endless twilight, sticky and green and dim. Massive trees fight for sunlight up above, filling every bit of air and making a dense canopy of leaves over the forest floor. Vines and plants hang from tree to tree like buttresses in a medieval church, and very little light can make it through. On the ground, little appears to move.

But for those who look closely, the entire forest is moving. Millions of bugs crawl on the ground and in the trees. Plants strangle each other in a battle for sunlight. Birds and small animals scurry from place to place to find food or some dark tangle of tree roots in which to hide from predators—pythons and jaguars and, deadliest of all, man.

Of course, Oliver and Celia were not watching closely and saw none of this.

They were tired and bored. The Amazon rain forest was dull, dull, dull.

Corey Brandt was loving it. It was like he had never had an adventure before. He raced from tree to tree. He held his little digital camera in front of him and spoke dramatically into it.

"I'm here in the Amazon at last, walking in the footsteps of the doomed explorer Percy Fawcett and the daring president Teddy Roosevelt. The distant cry of the monkeys shatters the great quiet of this emerald world. What is in store for us? Only nature knows for sure."

"Didn't we see a movie about Percy Fawcett and his son?" Oliver whispered to his sister.

"Yeah," she said glumly. "They vanished without a trace. Probably got eaten."

Oliver groaned. Sixth grade looked much more appealing now.

"We can give ourselves an advantage by masking our smells from predators," Corey continued into the camera with more enthusiasm than the moment seemed to require. "Watch!"

He set the camera down on some fallen leaves and dove down onto the damp ground, rolling around in the dirt.

"What are you doing?" Celia cried out. The teen star stood. He was filthy.

"I'm masking my scent like a hunter. Animals that track by smell won't know I'm here."

"Oh," said Celia, still not sure she understood why he would want to cover himself with mud. Sometimes the Celebrity Adventurist did things that made absolutely no sense.

"Um, Corey?" Oliver said. "I know you're the survival expert and all, but you . . . well . . . now you're covered in fire ants."

Corey Brandt looked down and saw that he was indeed crawling with hundreds of agitated fire ants. They were running up his legs and his torso, crawling toward his neck. He looked at his camera on the ground, still pointing up at him, filming.

"Eeep," he squeaked before turning on his heels and running toward the river as fast as his legs would carry him. A trail of ants followed on the ground.

"Don't jump in the water! That'll make them bite," Oliver yelled as Corey ran.

The twins gave chase. They caught up with the panicked TV star at the water's edge. He was frozen and still swarming with ants. They hadn't bitten him yet. He didn't move.

"What are you doing?" Oliver panted.

"I can't decide which is worse." Corey stared at the brown water of the river. "The ants or the piranha. What do I do?"

"You faced this before," Oliver said. "Remember? In the first season of *Agent Zero* you were taken prisoner by the Assassins' Guild and tied to a stake in the deserts of Kazakhstan. They smeared you with honey and sent the ants after you!"

"Oh . . . right . . . I . . . that was a while ago. . . . I've done a lot of shows since then. Could you, uh, remind me what I did to escape?"

"You took your clothes off," Celia answered. Oliver looked sideways at her. "What? He did. I remember that episode."

"You have to flick the ants off," Oliver said. "And, yeah, get out of your clothes and get away from them. Once you start flicking, they are going to get mad and bite, so you've got to move fast."

"I'm really glad you guys are fans." Corey took a deep breath. "And I'm glad I wore clean underwear."

Oliver and Celia stepped back. They didn't want the ants to turn on them. Fire ants could bite you a dozen times in a few seconds. "Ahh!" Corey screamed as he started flicking and tearing off his shirt and trousers. The ants started biting.

"Ow!" he yelled. "Ow!"

"Now run!" Oliver called.

Stripped down to his boxer shorts, Corey Brandt ran screaming into the jungle.

Oliver and Celia looked at each other, sighed, and gave chase.

"Slow down!" Oliver called out. "You don't need to run that far!" But Corey Brandt wasn't stopping for anything. One bite from a fire ant was enough for him for a lifetime.

They caught up to him back where he'd left his camera. He was standing in his boxer shorts, filthy, watching the playback on the tiny screen.

"With the right editing this could be pretty sweet," he said as the twins were catching their breath. Oliver set their backpack down and rested his head between his knees. He was not a fan of all this running.

"Sorry I lost my cool there," Corey said. "You guys were great. I'm really glad you pay such close attention to my shows. I'd be in real trouble out here without you."

"Uh . . . yeah. Corey . . . ," Celia said, catching her breath.

"Yeah?" He looked up at her.

"You probably . . . don't want . . . to stand . . . on the same anthill . . . again."

Corey looked down and saw that he'd gone right back to the spot he'd rolled in before and once again, fire ants were racing up his legs.

"Ahh!" he yelled and bolted back toward the river, holding the camera this time. He didn't stop at the water's edge when he got there. He just jumped in.

And so Celia and Oliver chased after the nearly naked celebrity through the jungle once more, leaping over fallen logs and tangled roots and branches that were bent and broken in strange patterns. They had never done so much sprinting in their lives.

This day, like so many of their days, was not going at all as expected, not for Oliver and Celia Navel, and not for the men watching them from the bushes, holding spears and blowguns at the ready.

24

WE ARE NOT MONKEYING AROUND

WHEN HE CLIMBED out of the pool at the base of the waterfall, Corey Brandt had a few angry welts on his skin where the ants had bitten him, and his perfect hair was wet, tangled, and dirty. The humid rain forest made drying his clothes impossible, so he was forced to put his shirt and pants back on wet, but at least there were no more ants crawling in them. Overall, it could have been a lot worse.

"I dove into a pool of piranhas!" Corey Brandt said. He was smiling. "This is so awesome!"

Oliver and Celia looked at him like he was crazy. If they were bitten by fire ants and jumped into a pool of piranhas and forced to wear soaking-wet clothes, they wouldn't find anything about it awesome. Hollywood must do weird things to a person's mind, thought Oliver.

"Exploring is so . . . *real*, you know? Well, you two know." He picked his camera off the ground and handed it to Celia. "Can you film for a second, Celia? I want to get some footage of my run-in with the fire ants."

"Sure," Celia said, hesitant, but happy to help. She liked hearing Corey Brandt say her name. He straightened his hair again. She hit the record button.

"Fire ants," Corey said loudly, his brow furrowed. His voice dropped deeper. This was his serious voice and it actually didn't sound much like him. Celia preferred when he just talked normally.

"They may look harmless, but as I've learned, they can swarm by the thousands and devour a human body in seconds. The pain of their bites is enough to drive a person mad." He smirked a little and the twins wondered if the bites had indeed driven him mad. He continued.

"Luckily, I remembered Corey Brandt's First Rule of Adventuring: Stay cool."

Oliver crossed his arms and frowned. Corey

Brandt didn't stay cool. Corey Brandt ran nearly naked through the jungle and jumped into a pool filled with piranhas.

It was Oliver and Celia who stayed cool.

"I also remembered that the proper response to a swarm of fire ants is full immersion in water. Even though the nearest pool was thick with piranha, I had no choice. I had to—" He looked over at Oliver. "What? What is it? Cut!"

Celia stopped filming. "What's wrong?" she said. She thought he'd been doing a great job.

"Your brother," Corey said. "He rolled his eyes."

"I did?" Oliver didn't even know he'd rolled his eyes.

"You did. You rolled them. What was it?" Corey Brandt scratched at the bites on his legs. "Was I too dramatic? Not dramatic enough? My acting coach always told me I needed to work my face more. Was there not enough face?"

"No, no," Oliver stammered. He had no idea how someone could not have enough face. What did that mean? "It's just that . . . ," he tried. "Well . . . you aren't supposed to jump into a pool of water when you're being attacked by ants. That makes them bite. I learned that from *your* show. I was just wondering why you didn't know it now when you knew it on TV? And, like, with the motorcycles. How come you don't know how to ride a motorcycle? On *Agent Zero* you got your learner's permit on a motorcycle."

"Well . . ." Corey didn't have an answer. He scratched at a bite on the back of his neck.

"You don't understand," Celia snapped at Oliver. "Hollywood isn't like school. You don't have to remember things after they're done, right, Corey?"

"Right," the star said. "Let's try that shot again," he suggested with a smile.

Celia held the camera up and Corey furrowed his brow again. He cleared his throat.

"Action," Celia said. She liked the sound of it. Maybe she was meant to be a TV director. It felt good to direct someone who wasn't her brother for a change. She hoped Corey would pull it together. She zoomed in on his face. He didn't have a freckle under his eye like a teardrop. Did he have a doctor remove it? Maybe he never had it to begin with; maybe he just had makeup artists put it on him so that little girls would get all mushy for him, just like Celia had. She started to feel angry at him.

She started to feel betrayed. She had really liked that freckle.

"Fire ants. They may look harmless, but as I've learned, the pain of their bites is enough to drive a person mad. In my own madness, I jumped into piranha-infested waters to escape the pain. I forgot Corey Brandt's First Rule of Adventuring: Don't jump into piranha-infested waters. It nearly cost me my life. Thankfully . . ." His voice choked up a little. "Thankfully, my friends were here to save me from myself." He stared at the camera for a moment in silence, like he was trying to think of something else to say. "Cut."

Celia lowered the camera.

She blew the hair out of her face. He called Oliver and Celia his friends. He said they'd saved him. Corey Brandt looked at them with tears in his eyes. Who needed a teardrop freckle, anyway? He was so—Celia searched for the word—vulnerable. Just like on *Sunset High*.

"How was that?" Corey asked Oliver.

Why was he asking what Oliver thought? Celia was the one who had been a fan of Corey Brandt's since he first appeared on TV with his sparkling eyes and vampire fangs. What did Oliver know about the art of cinema that Celia didn't?

"I think we should get a different angle," Celia said. "The, um, lighting wasn't good over here."

"The lighting's not good anywhere," said Oliver. "We're in the jungle."

"I know that!" Celia shouted. "I am just trying to make sure Corey gets the best show possible out of this. It'd be terrible if all our adventures were for nothing."

"Oh, so now you're an expert in reality television?" Oliver got right up in his sister's face. "Whenever I want to watch reality television, you tell me it lacks emotional depth."

"I never said emotional depth."

"Did too."

"Did not."

"Did too."

"Did not."

"Uh, guys?" Corey Brandt stepped between them and pointed up with one finger.

The three of them looked straight up to see a black jaguar pacing back and forth on the branch above them, staring down with hungry cat eyes.

"Why don't we . . . uh . . . keep moving," Celia suggested, dropping her voice to a whisper.

"Good idea," Oliver agreed.

Corey took the camera from Celia and filmed the panther as they backed away from it. Once they couldn't see it anymore, they turned and walked to where they'd left their backpack. Except it wasn't there.

"Could the ants have taken it?" Corey wondered.

"No," said Oliver. "It was a monkey."

"How do you know that?" said Celia.

"Because." Oliver pointed to a vine studded with white flowers. A gray monkey with a shock of black hair on its head hung off the vine about twenty feet in the air, and the monkey was holding their backpack. He screeched at them and swung from vine to vine, heading deeper into the jungle.

"Oh no," said Celia.

"More running?" said Oliver.

"Yep," said Celia, and off the trio raced after the monkey who had taken their backpack.

Celia, Oliver, and Corey ran below as the monkey raced along above them, swinging and leaping effortlessly through the canopy. It was hard going on the ground. Thorns, fallen logs, and tangled vines blocked their path. Oliver kept stumbling, so Celia took the lead.

Oliver was thrilled his sister was going first, but that only lasted until the first branch that she shoved out of the way snapped back and whacked him in the face.

"Ow! Watch it!" he yelled.

"I'm trying to watch the monkey!" She stopped in a small clearing and looked around at the trees, trying to see where the monkey went. "I think he went that way." She pointed and started to move, but Oliver grabbed her arm.

"We can't go that way."

"What? Why not?"

"Look at those bent branches." Oliver pointed at a bunch of branches that were bent back at impossible angles.

"So? There are broken branches in the jungle. What's your point?"

"Those branches are a sign. They're a warning that jungle Indians use. They mean 'no trespassing.'"

"Indigenous people," Celia said.

....

"What?"

"They're not called Indians. They're called indigenous people." She sang, *"If you are indigenous, the city feels vertiginous—"*

"Whatever," interrupted Oliver. "They're a warning that *indigenous people* use. We're still trespassing."

"But how do you know that?" Corey Brandt asked, filming the broken branches.

"Well," Oliver said. "You said it in *Agent Zero*, season one, episode nine: 'The Dictator in Gym Class.'"

Corey didn't look like he knew what Oliver was talking about. Something was definitely wrong with the star, but there was no time to question him.

"I also know because of the guy with the spear." Oliver pointed.

Celia and Corey turned and sure enough, there was a small man covered with black and red paint from head to toe, holding a spear up behind his head, ready to throw it at them. His dark black hair was cut into a bowl shape. His face was painted with complicated patterns of black ink, and the whites of his eyes shone out from his face in sharp contrast. He didn't move.

"Oh," Corey Brandt said, and swallowed hard. Suddenly, a dozen more warriors just like the first appeared all around them. They seemed to materialize from the shadows and the bushes and the earth itself. Some had spears and some had blowguns and none of them looked happy to see the Navel expedition.

Corey Brandt tried to smile at them with his winning smile, but the angry shout that came from behind him suggested that they were not his biggest fans. Celia felt suddenly weak in the knees—and it had nothing to do with Corey Brandt's smile.

She was thinking about being turned into dinner.

25

WE TAKE A HIKE

COREY, OLIVER, and Celia were led at spearpoint through the trees.

"Ow!" Celia stumbled over some tangled roots. "Stop jabbing me."

The man who had been jabbing her smiled widely. The smile did not mean he was being friendly. He was showing his teeth, which he had filed down to sharp points. If you have ever had a teeth cleaning at the dentist, you know how uncomfortable just a little scraping on the teeth can be. And this spear-poking gentleman's dental work was most assuredly not performed by a licensed dental professional.

The group was moving very quickly into the depths of the forest. Thorny branches tore at their clothes and tangles of vines choked their path.

The men made Corey Brandt tear the tangles of vines away in front of them with his bare hands.

"I can't believe this is happening," he said. Even though his hands were scraped and red, he was smiling. "Things just got *real*."

"That's not a good thing," Oliver groaned, and Celia couldn't disagree with him. It was events just like this that made the Navel twins dislike reality. No one ever got eaten while watching soap operas. She wondered what went on in Hollywood that made Corey Brandt love jungle torture so much.

Sometimes the hunting party would stop and crouch in silence. They pulled Oliver, Celia, and Corey down onto the ground, where they had a close-up view of thousands of bugs chewing and churning on the forest floor.

"Ew," Oliver said as his nose was pressed down next to a log crawling with termites.

They waited a few seconds and then continued on. Occasionally a man would stop and break the branch of tree, bending it back at an unnatural angle.

"A warning to anyone following us," Oliver said.

"So," Corey whispered. "Have you guys been in trouble like this before? I mean, like with your explorer family and all?"

"I guess," Oliver said with a shrug.

We might take this opportunity to note that on TV the same kinds of stories usually end the same way. The bad guy is caught; the monster is really still alive; the young couple kisses. If one watches enough TV, one always knows what will come next. But in real life, the past rarely makes promises about the future. Or, as Oliver might put it, just because you survive one deadly adventure with your sister doesn't mean you'll survive the next.

"You think these guys took your father?" wondered Corey.

"I hope not. There was an episode of *Celebrity Whisk Warriors* that tried to film in the Amazon," Oliver said. "The whole cast came down on a seaplane and walked into the jungle just like us. Everyone vanished. Even the seaplane vanished. They had to get a new host."

"*Celebrity Whisk Warriors*?" Corey helped hoist Oliver and Celia over a large fallen log. The warriors climbed over it effortlessly. "You watch cooking shows?"

"I guess so. You know . . . because of the . . . uh . . ." Oliver was actually grateful when one of the warriors poked him in the back to get him to be quiet. He didn't want the teen star to think he was weird. But he really did like cooking shows.

They walked for hours and hours. As they got deeper into the jungle, less and less light came through the treetops. They couldn't tell if it was because the sun was setting or because the canopy was getting thicker. Maybe it was both.

Oliver knew it had been over twenty-four hours since they'd eaten anything. He'd never been so hungry in all his life. Talking about *Celebrity Whisk Warriors* had made his mouth water. He hoped there would be food when they got where they were going. He also hoped that they wouldn't *become* food when they got where they were going.

26

WE GET WHERE
WE WERE GOING

THEY CAME OUT of the trees into a clearing
that was ringed by the jungle: the village of the
Cozinheiros. There was a long building in the
center, with one low door and a steep thatched roof.
Smaller huts spread out around it. A few fire pits
smoldered, but otherwise the village looked empty.
Now that they were out of the jungle, they could
see that the sun was beginning to set again. They
had hiked all day. They wondered if it was already
too late to save their father.

The men pushed Oliver, Celia, and Corey toward the long building. When they stepped over
the threshold, they were overwhelmed by the powerful smells of smoke and sweat. It took a second
for their eyes to adjust to the dim light, but once

they did, they saw that they were standing in front of the entire village.

Women and children were gathered at the far end of the long building, while a group of older men stood in a ring in the center. The older men all held spears, and all their spears were pointed at Corey Brandt and the twins. They shouted and threatened. The younger men who had captured them filed in behind and blocked any hope of escape.

The oldest man in the center stepped forward. He held a carved wooden staff with bright yellow feathers dangling from it and he waved it as he yelled at them. He must be the chief, thought Oliver. The chief always had a carved staff or something like that.

They had no idea what he was saying, but this was hardly the first time Oliver and Celia Navel had been yelled at in a language they didn't understand. It seemed like adults were always yelling at them in different languages. This was, however, the first time those adults might also eat them after they finished yelling.

Corey Brandt, who seemed not to notice the danger of their situation, pulled out his little cam-

era and started filming. The warriors rushed over to him and snatched the camera away.

"That is the property of Corey Brandt Productions!" he announced. "I am the leader of this expedition and I am responsible for these children. Release us immediately or you will be hearing from my lawyers!"

Celia rolled her eyes. The men murmured to each other and then pointed their spears at the celebrity. He slunk back and looked at his shoes.

"Okay, look," Celia said. "We don't want any trouble. We're just here to get our father back and be on our way."

"Your father?" a small voice said. From behind the wall of older men stepped a little girl about the same age as Oliver and Celia. They recognized her immediately. It was the llama girl who ran off in Machu Picchu.

"You!" said Celia. "You're not mute!"

"Of course I'm not," she said.

"Are you going to eat us?" Oliver gulped. "We're sorry we took your llama."

The girl just smirked. The chief spoke again. "He says you are trespassing on our territory," the girl translated.

"Are you the . . . um . . . Cozinheiros?"

"We have been called that," she said.

Oliver and Celia grabbed each other's hands.

"Did you kidnap our father?" Celia asked with a tremor in her voice. "We'd really like to negotiate for his release."

"That awful man with the mustache?"

"No, not him!" Celia shouted. "Although he got kidnapped too."

"Serves him right," the girl said. "But we didn't kidnap anyone."

"There were warriors," Oliver said. "They looked just like you. They kidnapped our dad from the town of Benjamin Constant."

"I fear," the girl said, "that you have been tricked. We do not go into Benjamin Constant, nor do we kidnap people." The chief spoke and several men pointed their spears and shouted. "You, however, are in big trouble. The chief says that you are with the destroyers."

"The destroyers?"

"Outsiders. They came with swords and metal helmets to burn our villages."

"That's the conquistadors," said Oliver. "But that was hundreds of years ago!"

"In the life of this forest, hundreds of years is a blink. The destroyers never stopped coming. They came with horses and swords and armor; they came with guns and airplanes; they came with cameras and microphones. Now they come with trucks and axes and they take our trees. Like that little man you were with. They sell our trees to make themselves rich."

"But isn't this a nature preserve?" Oliver asked. "The mayor of Benjamin Constant said no one was allowed in."

The girl just snorted at the mention of the mayor.

"The mayor is in business with the loggers. They cut down our trees and float them out on the river and the government looks the other way. Every tree is sacred to us, the way your fingers and your heart are sacred to you. They are part of us. They give us life and they make us who we are."

"A tree makes you who you are?" said Celia. That seemed pretty weird.

"They tell us stories. The flowers of the jacaranda tree tell us of the seasons changing. In the large roots of the *uacu* tree live the *bamberos*, mischievous spirits who are covered head to toe in hair. My family has told me stories of the *bambe-ros* since I was little, but they vanish with the trees. What stories will I tell my children?"

"We aren't here to take your stories," Celia explained. "We just want to rescue our father from whoever took him."

"Outsiders always brings calamity."

"Calamity?" Oliver whispered.

"Disaster," Celia snapped back. "Really, Oliver, you should know that one."

"How does *she* know that one?" Oliver pointed at the llama girl.

"*Wally Worm's Word World,*" the llama girl answered simply, as if it were obvious. "*If you find calamity, don't fall into insani—*"

The chief interrupted her with a loud cough.

The girl nodded and turned back to the Navel twins. "They wish to make an example of you," the girl said.

"An example?"

The llama girl pointed at Corey Brandt's camera, which one of the warriors was now using to record them.

"The chief has heard that cable news television likes exciting videos. He thinks showing your trial would be pretty exciting. And it would be better than breaking branches to warn off trespassers."

"Our trial?" Oliver thought about Judge Baxter. "Like in a court?"

"Sort of," the llama girl said. "It's more like a test. Or a game, even."

"But we didn't do anything!" Celia objected.

"I told them this," the girl explained. "That's why they are not spearing you to death right now. If you pass the trial, you will be accepted as fellow warriors and we will hold a feast in honor of your bravery."

"And if we don't pass?" Oliver wondered.

"There will still be a feast," the girl said sadly. "We are famous for our cooking, after all."

The man with the camera zoomed in on Corey Brandt's face. He did not give his famous smile. He looked like he was going to be sick.

"What's the trial?" Oliver asked.

"It's an ancient game my people have played with the rubber from our trees for centuries. I believe you call it dodgeball."

Oliver and Celia might have preferred being speared.

27

WE WOULD PREFER GREG ANGSTURA

OLIVER, CELIA, and Corey were shoved back outside. It was dark out. They heard the groans and growls of nocturnal predators in the forest beyond the clearing, which convinced them that trying to run would be a bad idea. Men holding torches formed a circle with Oliver, Corey, and Celia in the middle. The torchlight cast strange shadows across the painted bodies of the warriors. The rest of the villagers stood back, watching from the darkness. The man with the camera crouched in front of the warriors and zoomed in and out on the children's unhappy faces. He spoke to the llama girl.

"He says Corey Brandt looks older in real life," she translated.

"Oh, come on!" objected Corey Brandt.

Three warriors stepped into the circle holding three black rubber balls, each one the size of a baseball—and just as hard. This was going to be a lot more painful than sixth-grade recess.

"Well." Corey Brandt looked over at the camera. He pursed his lips in his practiced way. "This is what being a Celebrity Adventurist is all about, right?" He gave the camera a nervous thumbs-up. "Will you make sure he films my good side?"

The llama girl told the cameraman, who smiled to reveal his pointed teeth.

"I don't think they're worried about cinematography," Celia said.

"I'd just hate for my last TV appearance to look terrible."

Oliver rolled his eyes. He was now convinced that he liked Corey Brandt better on television than in real life.

"The rules are like this," said the llama girl. "The balls are placed in the middle of the circle. When I shout, you run and try to get a ball before the other side does. Then you throw it at them as hard as you can. You can use the whole circle to run around in, but you can't touch each other and you can't leave the circle. Whatever team still has a player standing at the end wins."

"And?" Oliver asked.

"That's it."

"But how do we get the other players out?"

"I said that. You throw the ball at each other as hard you can."

"And if we hit them they are out, right?" Celia finished the girl's thought.

The girl crossed her arms. She was getting annoyed. "Well, you can't knock them out without hitting them, can you?"

"Wait," Oliver said. "You mean, like, unconscious?"

"Yes. That's how you play dodgeball! Hit the other team until they can't get up anymore! I thought you all played this in your country!"

"We got kicked off the team," said Oliver. "For bad sportsmanship."

"Well, try to follow the rules here," the llama girl said. "Or they'll spear you."

That did sound worse than getting sent to Principal Deaver's office.

Celia rubbed her palms on her pants to dry

them. The warriors in the circle glared at them and crouched low, preparing to leap. They wore only loincloths to cover themselves, but their skin was decorated with patterns in black ink that made them almost dizzying to look at. The light from the torches flickered across their faces.

Oliver thought that it was unfair to put children up against three full-grown adults, but he didn't think his cries for justice would be answered, so he didn't bother. Arguing with the angry chief would be like arguing with Celia. It was better to save his energy for the challenge ahead.

A very old man, older than the chief, stepped into the circle. He wore a headband of turquoise stones and feathers and a necklace strung with animal bones. He shook a rattle in the air and chanted, tossing seeds around the edge of the circle. He was the shaman.

"The circle has been blessed," the llama girl said as the old man stepped back out, still chanting. Other men joined him in the chant.

"Oh, good," said Celia. "I'd hate to get bludgeoned to death in a circle that hadn't been blessed."

"Bludgeoned?" asked Oliver.

Celia just sighed; the llama girl nodded in understanding. She had brothers too.

She then gave a quick shout.

The game had begun.

Corey Brandt looked at the camera, gave a brave smile, and raced toward the center of the ring. Oliver and Celia looked at each other, a sad this-is-it kind of look, and rushed forward after him. Oliver felt everything go into slow motion, like at the end of a sports movie, except that instead of triumphant music there was only the creepy chanting of the crowd around him, waving their torches and spears in the air. Celia was determined to win. She ran faster than she'd ever run in her life. If only Mr. McNulty had threatened to eat the children, they would have given sixth-grade recess this kind of energy.

Of course, two eleven-year-old children and a teen television star are no match for experienced hunters of the tribes of the western Amazon. They spend their entire lives learning to run and throw. As we observed earlier, Oliver and Celia do all they can to avoid things like running and throwing. They did not make it to the center of the circle in time to get any of the balls.

The three warriors spread out around them, tossing the hard rubber spheres back and forth in their hands so their adversaries wouldn't know when they were coming.

"Hey, Oliver," said Celia, keeping her eyes on the warrior right ahead of her and poised to leap out of the way if he threw his ball at her.

"Yeah?" said Oliver, who had taken a different approach. He was running in circles around the edge of the ring without stopping.

"Remember Greg Angstura," she called out.

"Who?" said Corey, who was trying to stare down the warrior facing him.

Celia ignored him. "Remember what I did?"

"Yeah!" said Oliver, still running in circles. The warrior was getting dizzy trying to track him.

"Do it!" she shouted.

Oliver suddenly turned and ran right at the warrior, yelling, "Ahhh!" He raised his fist and punched straight up to hit the warrior right in the face.

The warrior didn't flinch. He looked down at Oliver and cocked his arm back with the ball.

"Dive!" shouted Celia.

Oliver dove to the side and the ball sailed over

him and slammed into one of the men on the edge of the circle, knocking him over. When the warrior across from Celia threw his ball, she hit the ground too. It also shot past her and whacked a man on the edge of the circle right in the stomach. He doubled over and fell.

"Hey, that's pretty goo—," said Corey Brandt as the third ball cracked him right on the head. He fell backward into the mud.

"Now's our chance!" Oliver shouted.

Celia turned and saw what her brother meant. The balls had knocked out two of the men on the edge of the circle, making two openings in the ring. Without a moment to lose, they each grabbed one of the teen's wrists and dragged him, running through the gaps in the circle. They used his body like a battering ram, knocking spectators out of the way. Chaos erupted.

"What the—?" Corey said, waking up with a groan. The twins dragged him to his feet just outside the circle.

"Run!" Celia shouted, pulling him along. They jumped over small children and weaved past the shocked elders, who realized too late that the trio wasn't planning on completing the trial. They were trying to escape into the jungle.

"Hey," the llama girl called out. "This is a test of bravery! You aren't supposed to run away! That's bad sportsmanship!"

28

WE ARE DOOMED, AS USUAL

THEY RACED THROUGH the clearing toward the dark forest beyond. In just a few strides, Corey Brandt was ahead of them, leading the way. Three rubber balls flew over their heads. Next came the spears.

"Come back and be brave!" the llama girl called out one last time. "Die with honor!"

The twins had no interest in dying at all, with or without honor. They needed to get away alive and figure out who had dressed up like this tribe and kidnapped their father. Could Sir Edmund have poison-darted himself to trick them? Could Janice McDermott have followed them to the Amazon? They really wished their mother were here to help. This seemed like a good time for her to reveal herself and explain things. But for now, they had to keep running. They were on their own.

They dodged into the dark forest, weaving between trees and vines. It wouldn't be long until the hunters were upon them. They took cover together under a giant tangle of tree roots that was taller than a full-grown man. They watched a group of barefoot hunters race past them, moving effortlessly through the dark.

"We should climb!" Oliver whispered. "They'll find us on the ground."

"I can't climb a tree," Corey Brandt said.

Oliver threw his hands in the air in exasperation. "But we just saw you climb a giant redwood on *The Celebrity Adventurist*! I learned the word *arboreal*!"

"I . . . um . . ."

"We know you don't do your own stunts," Celia said. "It's kind of obvious."

"Right," he said. "That's it. I'm sorry. I'm sorry I lied about doing my own stunts."

"It's fine," said Celia. "If Oliver and I can climb a tree, then anyone can, right? Now, let's go."

Oliver knew better than to argue with his sister, and it seemed Corey Brandt did too. They started climbing.

They climbed and shimmied like monkeys for a few minutes, reaching the canopy completely out of breath. When they couldn't reach a branch, Corey Brandt hoisted the twins up himself.

"That was great," he whispered. "You two are brilliant."

"Not really," said Celia. "It turns out, these guys know how to climb too."

The trio glanced down and saw that, indeed, they had been discovered, and eight warriors were climbing up trees all around them, moving very fast.

"You ever see any cartoons about the jungle?" Oliver asked.

"Which ones?" asked Corey.

"It doesn't matter," said Oliver. "Any story in the jungle has this part."

"Which part?"

"*This* part," Celia answered, looking glum and reaching for a vine hanging off the branch. "Get it?"

"We're gonna swing?" Corey Brandt looked nervously from twin to twin. They nodded. Corey grabbed on to the vine. Oliver and Celia grabbed on to Corey. They all sighed, and with one big push, the three of them swung free from the giant tree and flew through the air like trapeze artists. The warriors shouted after them.

Corey and Oliver also shouted. They squeezed their eyes shut while Celia scanned ahead for the next vine to grab.

"Boys," she announced. "I could really use your help grabbing on here."

As they swung, Celia caught on to the next vine, pulling it close enough for Corey to grab. Once they all had a grip, they let go of the first vine and swung again. It wasn't graceful but it worked. They were escaping faster than their pursuers could climb. They swung and swung from vine to vine. The twins' arms couldn't hang on anymore. They started to slip.

"Hang on!" Corey shouted at them. The twins gripped his shoulders as he swung them from vine to vine himself. The star of *The Celebrity Adventurist* was finally saving their lives.

As fast as they swung, the warriors had now caught on and were swinging behind them. Celia caught glimpses of them through the trees, moving from vine to vine far more gracefully than the three of them could manage.

"They're catching up!" she said.

One of the warriors swung straight at them from the front, cutting off the way they were heading. From the ground, warriors fired arrows at them, as two more came swinging in from each side. Corey caught on to a branch.

"Climb up!" he said. "I'll follow you."

The branches were thick enough for them to scamper through foliage and burst out into the open night sky. Moonlight lit the Amazon, and they stood and gazed out, three silhouettes on an ocean of rolling green.

"Whoa," said Corey. He smiled. He didn't seem so afraid of heights, Celia thought. But he was right; the sight was beautiful. Although they didn't have time to stay still and admire the view.

They moved quickly along the high branches, holding on to the thinner branches for balance. As they scurried, they saw the silhouettes of their pursuers pop up into the canopy. They ducked immediately and lay down on a wide branch, hoping they hadn't been seen.

The warriors called to each other in whistles,

organizing their hunt. Oliver closed his eyes and tried to be as quiet as possible. Celia looked around anxiously, fearing every moment that a dart from a blowgun would find her. Suddenly something touched her back. She gasped.

"Shh!" Oliver said.

Celia turned her head and saw a gray howler monkey with a shock of black hair perched next to her on the branch. The monkey cocked its head at her and reached out its rough black paw to stroke her cheek.

"Shoo," she whispered. "Go away."

The monkey picked at her hair and started grooming her, pulling tangles of vine and twigs from her pigtails. She tried to swat the monkey away with one arm, while the other stayed wrapped around the large branch. The monkey jumped back and cocked its head at her again. It scurried down into the canopy below. Celia let out her breath, relieved. They listened again to the darkness. The warriors whistled back and forth to each other, searching.

Suddenly the monkey was back on the branch next to Celia. And he was holding a backpack. He nodded at Celia.

"That's our pack!" Oliver whispered. "Give it back."

Much to the twins' surprise, the monkey opened the bag and pulled out the colorful bundle of knotted strings. He set the bag down and shoved it at Celia.

She tried to swat it away. "No, monkey, we don't need that now."

The monkey shoved it at her again. Finally, she took it from him.

"Okay? Now go away!"

The monkey patted Celia on the head and then disappeared into the canopy once more. Silence returned.

"That was weird," said Oliver.

"Shh," said Celia.

They heard nothing. Not even the whistles of their pursuers.

Then a noise shattered the silence.

"I'd show you something new, but your book is overdue . . ." Madam Mumu's voice echoed over the jungle. *"I'd show you something new, but your book is overdue . . ."*

"Sorry!" whispered Corey Brandt. "I thought it was broken."

"Silence it!" cried Oliver, but it was too late.

Three warriors appeared from below, surrounding the group. They whistled.

More warriors arrived. They were surrounded.

Corey pulled out his phone.

"You've got Corey," he whispered. "I can't talk right now. I'm about to be eaten."

One of the warriors snatched the phone from him and stared at the glowing screen. He swiped his fingers across it a few times and laughed. He showed the others how things moved when he touched it. They passed it from hand to hand and it quickly vanished.

"Hey!" Corey objected, but he was silenced by a poke in the back from a spear. "Okay . . . I can get a new one. No worries, guys. Enjoy."

Another warrior arrived, carrying the llama girl on his back. She stepped onto the thick branch where the twins and the celebrity were lying down.

"You failed the test of bravery," she said. "I guess you knew that."

The guy who'd carried her took Corey's camera from a small woven bag and started recording again. Corey straightened his hair.

"Are you going to spear us?" Oliver wondered.

"That's up to the elders," the llama girl said. "Probably. First we're going to take you back to the ground, where people belong."

Warriors moved forward and hoisted them to their feet, holding them firmly. Celia still clutched the old khipu that the monkey had returned to her. When they saw it, the warriors froze. The llama girl gasped. The man with the camera lowered it. No one moved.

"What?" Corey Brandt struggled in the grip of the warriors. "What's going on? Why'd he stop recording? Wait . . . is that the—?"

"How . . . ," the llama girl stammered. "Is it you?"

"Is *who* us?" Oliver wondered.

"I am sorry," the girl said to them. "For everything we have done. Do not be afraid. We will not hurt you. We have been waiting for you."

"Oh, what now?" Celia groaned. "Are we, like, the chosen ones or something?"

"Yes," the llama girl said. "Exactly that."

"Of course," Celia rolled her eyes. "Like always."

She really hated sudden twists of fate.

"So, Mnemones?" she said. "Lost cities? Ancient libraries? What is it this time?"

The llama girl just nodded.

"Well." Celia shook herself free from the warrior's grip. "Let's go down and get this over with. There'll be a prophecy, right?"

"There's *always* a prophecy," Oliver sighed.

"If it's not certain death, it's destiny." Celia tossed Oliver their backpack. "Why can't it just be, you know, normal?"

"First, we will feast in your honor," the llama girl added with a smile. "And we will help you find your parents."

"You mean our father?" said Celia.

"I mean *both* your parents," the girl said.

Oliver and Celia really wished they could skip the feast and go right to finding their parents. Even if they weren't on the menu, dining with cannibals was not their idea of a good time.

WE UPSET SOME
OTHER CHICKENS

BY THE TIME the warriors had helped Oliver, Celia, and Corey Brandt down from the high rain forest canopy, through the jungle, and back to the village, word had reached the chief of the remarkable turn of events. A bonfire blazed. The villagers were preparing a feast.

They ran up to Oliver and Celia, hugging them and pulling at their clothes, tugging at their noses and earlobes, laughing hysterically. Much to his dismay, they mussed Corey Brandt's hair. It should be noted that a simple handshake was not the way of greeting in their village. They got right into the children's faces and studied them in close-up. Just as Celia had imagined, it was awkward.

Oliver carried their somewhat tattered backpack, while Celia clutched the khipu to her chest tightly. That khipu had saved their lives and she wasn't about to let go of it now.

They were led to the *maloca*, which is what the villagers called the longhouse. Just outside, logs and stumps had been arranged in a circle and they were urged to sit. The elders emerged from the darkened opening of the longhouse, looking grave and thoughtful.

Women wearing grass skirts brought folded banana leaves to each of the children and to Corey Brandt. Their faces were painted with stripes and dots, and they wore necklaces of colorful stones and beads. Their hair was long and dark. It looked like they spent a long time working on their fashions, which was remarkable, because, other than the grass skirts, they wore little else. Oliver and Corey blushed. The women were not even the least bit embarrassed.

The women made eating motions. Celia glanced at the elders. None of their faces betrayed any emotion. They watched the visitors closely.

Oliver unfolded his leaf and saw that it contained a few blackened chunks of mysterious roasted meat.

"Uh, Celia," he whispered. "What do we do?"

"Eat!" the llama girl urged. "Eat or it will be a great insult."

"They're cannibals!" Celia whispered at her brother.

"The tabloids would go crazy if they knew about this," Corey Brandt said, holding a piece of the mystery meat between his thumb and forefinger.

"Couldn't we just eat bugs or something?" Celia asked. She hated eating bugs, but anything would be better than this. She wished their mother were here. She would know what to do. She must have dined with cannibals a thousand times. Was this why she had made sure they got that khipu? Did these cannibals know her? Did they know where she was?

"It's good," the llama girl said. "A great delicacy." She nudged them on. "It was very hard to . . . catch." She smirked.

The rest of the village was staring at them. Smiles faded from the women's faces. The chief whispered something to one of the warriors, who nodded and clutched his blowgun.

"Oh boy," Oliver said to himself as he lifted up a small piece of meat from the banana leaf.

"Oliver, *what* are you *doing*?" Celia's eyes widened at her brother.

"When in the Amazon, do as the Amazonians do," he said.

He shut his eyes, held his nose, and dropped the piece of meat into his mouth. It was moist and rich. A little burned, but in a way he liked. It was horrifyingly delicious. As her brother chewed, Celia stared at him with her mouth wide open.

"You just . . . ," Corey Brandt said, and fainted.

"Well?" asked the llama girl as Oliver swallowed.

"Tastes like chicken," Oliver said. He opened his eyes and looked at the stern faces watching him. He turned to the llama girl. "Who . . . who was it?"

"She had no name," the llama girl said sadly. Oliver's stomach did a somersault. "Because she was a chicken!"

The girl burst out laughing. The entire village did the same. The chief had to lean on one of the warriors for support because he was laughing so hard. The trees shook with laughter.

"But—," said Oliver.

The llama girl looked up at Oliver, still shuddering with laughter. "We don't eat *people*," she said. "We aren't cannibals!"

"But—," Oliver repeated.

"Long ago, there were tribes that would eat parts of their enemies after a battle, and so stories of cannibals spread from the jungle to the lands beyond. Outsiders spread these stories about the natives of the forest to make us seem like savages. Now we allow the stories to continue for our own reasons."

"To scare people away," Celia said, understanding. "To protect your land."

"That's right," the girl explained. "Sometimes a myth is far more powerful than a spear. Look at what it did to Mr. Corey Brandt." She pointed at the unconscious actor on the ground. "You know, he looked shorter on *Sunset High*."

"I know!" said Celia. "I liked that Annabel was taller than him. It was romantic."

"I still think he should have ended up with Lauren," said the llama girl. "They had so much more in common. Annabel was holding him back. Lauren would have become undead for him."

"Annabel was his destiny!" Celia objected.

"But . . . ," Oliver said again, still in shock.

His sister seemed suddenly to remember her brother was there. "I can't believe you ate that when you thought it was people."

"Well, it wasn't people, was it?" he told her, and ate the rest of his chicken. Celia shook her head again and dug into her own meal. She ate quickly while she and the llama girl talked about their favorite episodes of *Sunset High*.

The other villagers joined in the chicken feast. Corey Brandt was eventually revived. They had to explain to him all over again that they weren't cannibals. Still, he claimed to be a vegetarian and would only eat the sweet potatoes that the women had roasted.

"Just like Annabel," said the llama girl, and she and Celia burst into fits of laughter. Oliver just looked at the actor and shrugged.

When the meal was done, the old shaman stood and, with one gesture, the entire village grew silent. He began to speak. A few of the village children shifted uncomfortably on the ground or plucked at the dirt by their feet. It kind of reminded Oliver and Celia of the Ceremony of Discovery back at the Explorers Club, when all the scientists and adventurers gave speeches.

The chief sat on a log off to the side with the rest of the warriors. Whatever was about to happen was not up to him. He handled the normal affairs of the village, like organizing marriages and hunting parties, settling disputes, and fighting off intruders. The shaman—like shamans all over the world, whether they are high in the Himalayas, deep in the Amazon rain forest, or nestled in the VIP room of a celebrity fitness club in Los Angeles—was responsible for the link between the spirit world and the physical world. He was the keeper of prophecy, and it was his turn to speak.

"You have the Inca's Itinerary," the llama girl translated for the shaman. "We have long awaited its return."

"Sure you have," Celia interrupted. "How come our janitor had it?"

"Custodian," whispered Oliver.

"What?" his sister snapped at him.

"The right way to say it is custodian. Even I know that, and I don't have a rhyme for it."

"Right, okay. Sure. Custodian," she said. "How come our custodian had it?"

"Destiny," she said. "We were told long ago that two explorers would bring it back to us."

"We are not explorers!" Celia objected. "We just want to find our father and get cable TV and go back to the sixth grade without getting killed."

"Whatever you are, or think you are, does not matter. You are here now, and you have brought our itinerary back to us."

The shaman and the llama girl talked back and forth for a moment. It sounded like an argument.

"What?" Celia said. "What's he saying?"

"There is much you do not understand," the girl answered. "Your path ahead is dangerous."

"Of course it's dangerous," said Celia. "It's *always* dangerous."

"You will have to make a choice."

"A choice about what?" said Oliver.

"A choice about your destiny."

"We just want our parents back," said Celia. "We don't care about destiny."

The llama girl put her arm around Celia's shoulder. "Do you know what a vision is?"

30

WE GET SOME TV TIME

OLIVER AND CELIA knew all too well what a vision was. In Tibet they had been forced into a deep, dark pit and their only way out was to meditate and try to have a vision. They still weren't sure it worked, because some kid who might also have been a vision himself interrupted them. He saved their lives. Or he put their lives in more danger. They couldn't be sure. This vision business was complicated.

"Yeah," Celia said. "We know what a vision is. It's like television. Only the tele- part is in your mind."

"Close enough," said the girl. The shaman produced a bowl filled with some sort of potion. Some of the village men started to sing and pound on drums.

The shaman passed the bowl around the circle of villagers and each drank from it and the shaman refilled it when they were done.

"This is the Vine of the Soul," the llama girl explained. "It is our way of summoning visions, a potion that will unlock for you the mysteries you seek."

"Like where our father is?" Celia asked.

"Like where our mother's gone?" Oliver wondered.

The llama girl didn't answer. She simply helped the shaman fill the bowl with liquid and take it to everyone who had chosen to sit in the circle, young and old.

When the bowl reached Oliver, he drank the potion down without hesitating. For the second time, Celia stared at him with her mouth agape. The shaman chanted more loudly.

"It is okay," the llama girl said. "If you do not wish to unlock the mysteries, you may simply sit and wait with the others."

Celia was through with sitting and waiting and not understanding anything. She drank the potion and closed her eyes. It was bitter and thick and it made her stomach hurt. Next to her, Oliver looked pale too. Corey Brandt waved the bowl away. He stood and left the circle.

Celia suddenly doubted the wisdom of drinking strange jungle potions, but the shaman began to dance and shake the rattle in his hand and Oliver and Celia began to feel very strange.

Oliver tried to stand and walk over to a hammock he'd seen in the longhouse, but his legs felt like cooked noodles.

"Noodles," he mumbled as he felt himself being carried. He suddenly felt very, very sleepy.

Celia wasn't sure why she was so tired all of a sudden, but she was happy when she felt hands lift her from her seat and carry her to a hammock next to her brother, who was sound asleep.

The llama girl and the shaman stayed by their sides; the chanting grew louder and faster. The llama girl held the khipu in the air and the shaman ran his fingers over it, murmuring.

That's when Celia's dream began. Or maybe it was Oliver's dream. He was there too, and he looked just as confused as his sister. Oliver always looked a little confused, though, so it was hard to tell.

"Did I just say noodles?" he asked.

"Yeah," said Celia.

"Are we asleep?"

"I think so."

"Is that why we're back in Tibet?"

"Oh," said Celia, looking around. They were back in Tibet, standing on a snowy cliff, with the llama girl, the shaman, and a large stinky yak. "What are we doing here?"

"It is your dream." The shaman shrugged, catching some snow on his tongue. "I am not sure that I like the cold."

"We should go inside," the llama girl said, and a house seemed to appear from the snow high above them on the edge of a steep cliff.

"Do we have to climb in our dreams too?" Oliver groaned.

"Just go up," said Celia. "Let's get this whole vision thing over with."

They began to climb, straight up. They stretched and strained for tiny toeholds and handholds and struggled not to look down.

If you ever find yourself scaling the jagged rocks of a treacherous cliff face, remember this advice: do not look down. Many a great climber has made the error of looking down. The sight of great height and the realization of one's smallness in the face of gravity have overwhelmed more than one of these climbers, and the results have been disastrous.

Oliver and Celia looked down.

They were impossibly high up. Oliver's leg started bobbing like a sewing machine needle. Celia froze in place.

She wondered what would happen if they fell off a cliff in their dream. Would it ruin the vision? Would they fall in real life? Would they never wake up?

"Keep climbing!" she told her brother, and, never one to question his sister's wisdom while hanging off a cliff thousands of feet in the air, he kept climbing.

"We even have to exercise in our dreams?" he muttered as he climbed. "This is totally unfair."

The llama girl and the shaman were already standing outside the house when Oliver and Celia reached the top. Somehow they had not needed to climb with Oliver and Celia.

"Totally unfair," Oliver repeated.

They opened doors for the twins and showed them inside.

They were in their apartment back at the Explorers Club. Beverly sat on the sofa in front of the television. The monkey who'd stolen their backpack sat next to her.

"Fancy a spot of telly?" Beverly said with a thick British accent.

"Oliver?" Celia asked. "Why is your lizard talking?"

"She's not my lizard," said Oliver. "And anyway, you tell me. It's your dream."

"How do you know it's my dream?"

"Because I would never dream about Corey Brandt," he said. Corey Brandt was sitting in an armchair across the room, wearing a tuxedo.

"It's not my dream," he said. "I'm not even here. I don't even know you."

Then he went to the Cabinet of Count Vladomir, which sat next to their refrigerator, and stepped inside, vanishing into a strange forest that the twins were pretty sure did not usually exist inside their parents' antique furniture.

"Strange," said Celia. "He had his freckle back. Under his eye."

"*That's* what was strange?" Oliver shook his head at his sister. Girls.

"Ahem," said the lizard. "A spot of telly?"

"Pushy lizard," said the llama girl.

"They all are," said Oliver.

Celia found herself suddenly holding the remote control. She turned on the television.

They saw their father on the screen. He was lying on an ugly plaid couch in the living room of an unfamiliar house. He was talking to someone sitting in an ugly plaid chair.

"I just can't believe this," he said. "I can't believe you would do this to the children." He was pale and sweating, like he was sick. He was shaking his head back and forth. "I can't believe you would do this to *our* children."

The image on the screen changed to the person in the chair. A close-up on her face.

"Mom!" said Oliver.

"Mom?" said Celia.

"Oggie," she said, resting her hand on their father's knee. She was the only person in the world who called him Oggie. "I had to do it," she said.

"You left us, Claire. You left us for three years."

"I had to leave you. There is an ancient battle going on and Oliver and Celia are the only ones who can win it."

"The library?"

"That's part of it," she said.

Oliver and Celia looked at each other in surprise. The Lost Library was only part of it? What were the Council and the Mnemones really searching for?

"They're only children," their father said. "They can't do this. They watch too much TV. They complain about everything. They aren't cut out for the lives we imagined for them."

"Oh, so now you notice?" said Oliver sarcastically. Beverly and the monkey glared over at him.

"They are amazing explorers. Better than you or I," their mother said. "That's why I had to kidnap you and Sir Edmund."

"Mom did this?" exclaimed Oliver.

"She's done worse," said Celia.

"I don't understand," their father said.

"The guardians would never have shown themselves to an entire expedition, especially not one filled with explorers. And Sir Edmund *could not* be allowed to know their secrets, no matter what. So I had to get the children into the jungle on their own." She leaned closer to her husband. "They are going to find El Dorado, Oggie. They are going to find the Lost Library."

"But you know how dangerous that is! How many explorers have died in that very search? This is madness!"

"I know," their mother said. "But they are the only ones who can."

"It's just a library, Claire. A really old library!"

"It's what the library contains that is so important," she said. "I can't explain it all to you now, but trust me. The fate of the entire world is at stake."

"Oh, come on!" Oliver shouted at the TV. "We have to save the world now?"

Beverly shushed him again.

"We left them with that actor," a man said, entering the room. It was Professor Rasmali-Greenberg, wearing a tweed suit and a purple bow tie with orange ducks on it. "He's the Adventuring Celebrity, so they should be fine."

"Celebrity Adventurist," their father corrected him. At least he paid attention. "And he's only a child himself."

"He looked older in person," the professor said.

"The twins will know what to do." Their mother looked briefly toward them, as if she could see through this tiny TV screen, as if she knew they were watching. Celia thought she saw their mother smile.

Suddenly, a new voice entered the scene.

"I think I'd like you to tell me where they are," it said.

It was Sir Edmund, standing in the doorway to the living room.

"And Professor," he said, "I do not appreciate how you have treated me. I think I shall be resigning from the Explorers Club on account of this betrayal."

"How did you get out of the closet?" Claire Navel demanded.

"Oh, some of my friends arrived." Sir Edmund smiled as the mayor of Benjamin Constant and a group of burly loggers entered the room, all of them armed with clubs and rifles. Behind them stood Principal Deaver, smiling cruelly and holding Beverly at the end of a purple satin leash.

"Oh, dear me," said Beverly in their dream. "How embarrassing!"

"I should very much like to know the whereabouts of your children," Principal Deaver said. "I'm concerned for their safety. And for yours."

Just then, the image filled with static and the scene was gone.

"What happened?" Celia asked, shooting to her feet. "What's going on? Was that real?"

The shaman held the khipu in the air and spoke. The monkey screeched. This time, Beverly translated with her thick British accent while the llama girl sat with her eyes closed and listened.

"The Sweet Sea forks into darkling waters," the lizard said.

"Darkling?" Oliver whispered at Celia. She just shrugged.

"Ahem!" Beverly coughed. "It's rude to interrupt. I may be just a dream, but I have feelings."

"Moody lizard," Oliver muttered.

"Darkling waters," Beverly continued. "Beyond the serpent's tongue and through weeping trees, where doubt itself bends toward a shadow, there the knight should boldly ride, if he seeks for El Dorado."

The image on the TV changed from static to a ruined city in the jungle, overgrown with vines and trees, but the screen zoomed in on a wall at the base of the building, where a tiny glimmer of gold caught the sunlight. It was a golden key engraved on the wall.

The twins knew the symbol immediately: the Mnemones.

Then the image turned back to the strange living room, where Sir Edmund's thugs were tying up Oliver and Celia's parents and the professor. The screen changed once more to a water tower with the smiling face of Velma Sue, of Velma Sue's snack cakes, on it. The screen went to static.

The shaman stopped chanting. Beverly scurried away. The apartment itself seemed to melt from the walls inward, leaving the twins lying in hammocks in the longhouse in the village of the Cozinheiros. A pool of quicksand formed below the TV and it began to sink. As the last flicker of static vanished into the quicksand, Oliver and Celia woke up.

It was daylight.

"What . . ." Oliver rubbed his head. "What was that?"

"You have had a vision," the llama girl said. "You have seen the truth."

"We saw our mother and father," said Celia.

Oliver looked at the khipu. "Does this thing really say all that stuff about darkling waters and shadows of doubt and stuff? Is that the way to El Dorado?"

"Sort of," the llama girl explained. The shaman gently took the khipu from Celia and counted out knots on his fingers. "This is the Inca's Itinerary. It describes all the places along the way to the City of Gold that the Inca traveled in the past. As their civilization was destroyed, the last Inca rulers hid in the jungles. My ancestors. We were taken in by the Cozinheiros. We were given shelter, and they agreed to guard our secret places. El Dorado—which means 'the gilded one'—was such a place."

"Gilded?" Oliver asked.

"Covered in gold," Celia said.

"How—oh, right. The Worm."

"If you cover it in gold, then it's gilded, so I'm told," the llama girl said. "Anyway, our ancestors had hidden something very important in that place and the conquistadors would stop at nothing to get it. We spread all kinds of false stories about the city so no one would ever know what was really there, but it seems that some explorers have figured it out."

"Is it the Lost Library of Alexandria? Is that where it was hidden?" Celia said.

The llama girl nodded. "Our shamans are the only ones who know how to read these strings to find it, and that is why your mother wanted you to come here."

"So we could learn how to read these strings?" said Oliver.

"So we could show you, yes," the girl explained. The shaman spoke and she translated again. "Each knot is a distance. The colors are different places and directions. You read it with your fingers and your eyes, just like you would read the world." The old man counted knots on the string and pointed to the different places in the forest beyond.

"So what about our parents?" Celia asked. "What did we see there?"

"You saw another path," the girl translated. "You saw what you needed to see so that you may choose your destiny."

"Our destiny involves a living room filled with Velma Sue's snack cakes?"

"It appears so," the llama girl said. "We can take you to this place. We can help you rescue your parents, if that is what you choose."

"I don't think that's going to happen," said Corey Brandt, suddenly standing in the doorway to the longhouse.

"What? Corey? Where have you been?" asked Celia.

"We're going to find this 'gilded one,'" he said. "We're going to El Dorado."

"We have to save our mom and dad," said Oliver.

"You do what you want," he said, and reached into the pocket of his pants to remove a small pistol. "But I'm going to discover the Lost Library and sell it to the highest bidder."

"Corey," Celia cried. "What are you doing?"

"Corey, Corey, Corey," he sighed. "And they said I wasn't convincing . . ."

"Who said . . . what?" Oliver murmured.

The horrible realization hit Celia like a dodge-ball to the face.

"You are missing a freckle," she shouted. "You're not Corey Brandt!" She had noticed the missing freckle but convinced herself it didn't matter. She had noticed that he looked older and taller in real life, but she had convinced herself that the camera made people look shorter.

It didn't.

Movie stars were always shorter in real life. She knew that. She wanted so badly to believe that Corey Brandt would want to travel the world with them, would want to be their friend, that she ignored all the signs. This guy had never even watched Corey's shows.

"You're the guy who was kicked off *Dancing with My Impersonator*!" she said.

The impersonator smiled at her. "Unfairly kicked off," he said. "I'm the perfect Corey Brandt impersonator. I do mall appearances and birthday parties and no one ever complained . . . until that stupid TV show."

"You're not perfect," said Oliver. "The real Corey Brandt can do his own stunts. And you almost got eaten by ants! You don't know how to ride a motorcycle. And you're too tall and too old. You're nothing like Corey Brandt!"

"I am not too old," the impersonator sneered. "I am only twenty-six."

"What have you done with the real Corey Brandt?"

"You'd have to ask my partner that one. She did the dirty work there."

"She?" said Celia. "You don't work for Sir Edmund?"

"Janice," groaned Oliver as he realized. "You're in cahoots with Janice McDermott!"

"Really now, Oliver, who says cahoots?" said the fake Corey Brandt.

"That's who was on the phone!" Celia shook her head. "I knew it. I knew Corey Brandt didn't have a personal shopper! He said so on *Celebrity Access Tonight*." She smacked herself in the forehead. All that pointless Corey Brandt trivia she knew could have saved them, if only she hadn't been so starstruck.

"I told him to study the details," a woman said as she stepped from the shadows, climbing over sleeping tribesmen and pointing her rifle at the twins, the llama girl, and the shaman.

It was Janice McDermott, back for revenge.

She looked different than she had the last time they saw her, when she was disguised as a Tibetan mountain climber at the Explorers Club. Now she wore camouflage and had a big backpack on her back with pickaxes and chisels and a belt of bullets around her waist—all the tools of the grave robber's trade. Her hair was short and black.

"You'll never get away with this," said Celia. "The world will search for the real Corey Brandt."

"And they'll find him," said the impersonator. "I'll *be* him."

"And I'll have found the Lost Library and avenged Frank Pfeffer's untimely demise," added Janice. "A happy ending for everyone . . . except the Navels. And the real Corey Brandt." She shrugged. "As lovely as it is to see you both again, I think your friends are waking up, and I don't want to end up eaten like poor Frank."

"They're not really—," Oliver started, but Celia shushed him.

The fake Corey Brandt snatched the khipu from the shaman's hands and he and Janice McDermott slipped out of the longhouse. The villagers were just starting to emerge from their own strange dreams. Even the llama girl tugging at them and the shaman shaking his rattle couldn't rouse them faster.

Oliver and Celia ran outside.

Just before Janice and her partner vanished into the jungle, the Corey Brandt impersonator looked back at them with a wink and smile.

Celia was as unimpressed as the game show judges.

31

WE TAKE A PATH

"**SO WHAT DO WE** do now?" asked Oliver. "Do we chase them?"

"They have guns," said Celia.

"They took the thingy," said Oliver.

"Khipu," said Celia.

"I know," said Oliver.

"Your vision showed you two paths," said the llama girl. "The City of Gold and your parents. Your parents are in danger, as is the City of Gold. You must decide which is more important: your parents or the quest for—"

"Our parents," the twins said before she'd even finished speaking.

"We want to go rescue our parents," said Celia. "We don't care about El Dorado or the Lost Library. That's Mom's thing."

"But in your vision, your mother said the fate of the world was at stake."

"She can be kind of dramatic," said Oliver. "She's an explorer. And anyway, if someone needs to save the world, it's better our parents than us. We're more, like, indoor kids."

"We'll need your help," said Celia. "We can't fight our principal and Sir Edmund alone."

"All right," the llama girl said. "We will take you to this place with the snack cakes and the plaid furniture. We will help you rescue your parents."

"Is it a long hike there?" Oliver asked. He was pretty tired after a day of hiking, dodging, running, climbing, and then a night of weird visions.

"Don't worry," said the llama girl. "We'll take our plane."

"Your plane?" Celia exclaimed. "You have an airplane?"

The llama girl shrugged. "It's not exactly *our* plane," she said.

It was a short hike to reach the seaplane. It was tied to a tree at the river's edge, hidden from view by layers of moss and leaves and vines. A giant whisk and chef's hat were painted on the side.

"This is the plane from *Celebrity Whisk Warriors*," Oliver said.

"That's right," the llama girl answered. "People leave all kinds of things behind when they are running for their lives."

"Why did you chase them off? They could have made your tribe famous."

"They never asked our permission to come here," the llama girl said matter-of-factly. "Not everyone wants to be on reality TV."

Oliver and Celia couldn't imagine that, but these days, the unimaginable had started to seem pretty normal. Their mother had abducted their father with a poison dart, and they had just had a vision of their parents discussing their fate in a quaint suburban living room in the middle of the jungle, so why couldn't there also be people who didn't want to be on TV? Anything was possible.

"Do you know how to fly it?" Oliver asked.

"We've never needed to," said the llama girl.

Oliver looked over at his sister.

She looked him right in the eye. "No," she said.

"Oh, come on!"

"It's not the same."

"How different could it be?"

It was the llama girl's turn to be confused. "What? How different could what be? What are you talking about?"

"Celia knows how to fly a plane," Oliver told her.

"I do not," Celia objected. "I've just watched *Love at 30,000 Feet* a lot of times."

"You have every episode memorized."

"So?"

"So you've seen Captain Sinclair take off a hundred times. You even know the episode where he gets knocked out by the bird flu while his copilot is in a Norwegian prison and the Duchess in Business Class has to fly the plane. And she can't read! If she can fly a plane, you can fly a plane!"

"Yeah, but it's not the same . . . that's a 747! This is a seaplane."

"Do you want to save Mom and Dad?"

"Yeah."

"Do you want to get our family back together?"

"Yeah."

"Do you want to get out of this jungle and get cable?"

"Yeah."

"Then you're gonna have to try."

Celia considered her options. No one else knew how to fly a plane and she wasn't about to let Oliver try. On the shows he liked, every plane crashed. There was even a show called *Plane Crash!* that he never missed.

"Fine," she said. "But no backseat flying."

Before they could board the plane, the shaman pulled a small gourd from a pouch around his neck and dipped his finger in it. It was covered in dark black ink. He painted dots on Celia's forehead and a series of stripes on Oliver's face.

"Now you are ready," the llama girl explained. "You go into battle with us."

They boarded the plane with half a dozen of the warriors.

Celia was in the pilot's seat and the llama girl sat next to her to be the navigator. Oliver found himself squeezed in between the warriors in the back. Their large arms squished him into himself. Their spears and blowguns and bows and arrows were piled every which way. They all sat perfectly still and quiet.

If Oliver didn't know that they were deadly jungle hunters, he would have thought they were nervous about flying.

They were.

Outside the plane, the shaman chanted blessings. Celia pulled on knobs and levers. She flipped switches that made the plane groan and beep. She found a starter and hit it and the propeller on the nose of the plane churned to life, breaking free of vines and moss as it spun faster and faster.

"Engines. Check," Celia said, because that's what Captain Sinclair said on the show. She was going to do everything she could just like TV and hope they would have a happy ending. Flying a plane full of tribal warriors to a ruined suburb in the jungle where she would rescue her parents from her principal was not the way she had expected to spend the first week of sixth grade. She let out a slow breath.

"Here we go," she said. "The captain has turned on the 'fasten seat belts' sign. Prepare for takeoff."

She steered the plane to the center of the river and pulled back on the throttle. The acceleration pressed Oliver against his seat and pressed the warriors against Oliver. The plane lifted off the river.

If they survived this flight and saved their parents, Celia thought, they'd better get cable television.

32

WE'VE GOT A GAMBIT

IN THE BEDROOM of the house in the jungle, Claire and Ogden Navel were having a long-awaited reunion. They were tied back-to-back on two dining room chairs and locked in the closet. It was dark and sticky, but they were happy to be together again.

"I forgot how much more I enjoy danger when you're around," Dr. Navel told his wife.

"That's good," she said, "because there is plenty of it."

"I am still a bit mad at you for kidnapping me and putting our children's lives in danger."

"There's no how-to manual for parenting, Oggie. I'm doing the best I can."

"I know . . . I know . . ." Dr. Navel was quiet for a moment. "So what is this place anyway?"

"This is Velma Sue's Snack Cakeville," she said, as if that explained anything.

"Oh," said Dr. Navel. He had no idea what Velma Sue's Snack Cakeville was, but he hated to admit that to his wife.

For those of us who are not embarrassed by what we don't know, I'm happy to elaborate on the subject of Velma Sue's Snack Cakeville, based on my extensive research into the history of the snack cake industry.

Snack Cakeville is a town in the heart of the Amazon rain forest built by Minnesota baker, housewife, and industrialist Velma Sue Harrison. In the early twentieth century, Velma Sue invented her delicious snack cakes by discovering a secret ingredient that gave them an extra-special taste and bounce—all-natural rubber. Rubber trees grew wild in the Amazon rain forest and Velma Sue believed she could make a lot of money if she built a snack cake factory right in the Amazon where the rubber grew.

To accompany her factory, she decided to build a model American town to go with it. If her snack cakes were to be wholesome and good, then her factory town should be too, she thought.

She built American-style houses and a water tower and a movie theater and an ice cream parlor and a schoolhouse. She thought she could tame the jungle.

Of course, the jungle had other plans. The experiment was a failure; the factory closed. The town was abandoned. The wilderness took it back. She changed her secret ingredient.

Dr. Claire Navel had found the abandoned town to be a very comfortable hideout.

Until, of course, Sir Edmund's Council found it.

The Navels heard Sir Edmund and Principal Deaver talking in the next room.

"I am certain the twins will come here," he explained. "And when they do, we'll have the whole family lead us to El Dorado."

"How can you be sure they even know where we are?"

"They are resourceful, in spite of themselves."

"That is my worry," Principal Deaver answered. "If they have already translated the khipu, why wouldn't they seek out El Dorado first? If the library is really there and they are to find it, all our plans could . . ."

Sir Edmund laughed. "They couldn't care less about the Lost Library. They're children. They don't even like books. They just want their mommy back."

In the dark closet, Claire Navel cringed. Dr. Navel reached his hand back as much as he could against the ropes that bound him and touched her on the wrist.

"Am I a horrible mother?" she asked.

"You did what you thought was best," he said. "But neither of us will win any parenting awards."

"No great explorer would. Discovery is a dangerous business."

"When this is over, maybe we should settle down, let the kids have normal lives."

"I'm not sure I know how."

"Me neither," said Dr. Navel. "But I do wonder if all this is worth it. To find a library?"

"It's not just a library, Oggie. It's something that the scholars in Alexandria found. It's what's *in* the library. And it's what would happen if Sir Edmund and his people find it first. I wish I could explain it all to you."

"You could try."

"Not right now, honey," she said. "Right now, we're going to escape."

She stood up, letting a frayed bundle of rope fall to the floor.

"How did you—?"

She smiled and held up her ring with the symbol of the Mnemones on it. A tiny blade was popped out. "There's also a little magnifying glass, but you need another magnifying glass to see it," she said as she untied her husband. "No ropes can keep a mother from protecting her kids."

"I suppose we should wake up the professor," said Dr. Navel. Professor Rasmali-Greenberg was sound asleep in the back of the closet buried under a pile of moldy coats. His arms and legs were tied, but he didn't seem the least bit uncomfortable. In fact, he didn't like having his nap interrupted.

"Five more minutes?" he groaned.

"Time to escape," Claire Navel said.

She helped him to his feet and the three explorers huddled together.

"I have a plan," she told them. "Do you remember the Zanzibar Gambit?"

"You're not thinking—" Dr. Navel's voice became hoarse.

"I am. Do you remember it?"

"Sadly, yes," said Dr. Navel. "But we don't have the supplies for that."

His wife pulled a handful of rubber bands and a whistle from her pocket.

"What about the steamer trunk?"

"On the other side of the door."

"Sack of flour?"

"In the pantry off the kitchen."

"Garden spade?"

"In the garden, of course!"

"And the monkey with a crowbar?"

Just then they heard a thump and the closet door slid open. The logger who had been guarding them was unconscious on the floor.

A small gray howler monkey with a shock of black hair stood on the man's chest holding a crowbar proudly in the air. He smiled a wide monkey-toothed grin.

"Meet Patrick," Claire Navel said. "He's the finest monkey I have ever known."

"Claire?" said Dr. Navel.

"Yeah?"

"It's nice to have you back." He wrapped his arms around his wife and kissed her. She held his face in her hands, staring at him with a smile.

"Pardon the interruption," the professor said. "But might I ask, why do you need rubber bands, a steamer trunk, a sack of flour, a garden spade, and a monkey with a crowbar?"

"You forgot the whistle," said Claire Navel.

"Yes," added the professor. "And a whistle?"

"For the Zanzibar Gambit," answered Claire Navel.

"But *what is* the Zanzibar Gambit?"

"Well, Professor," said Dr. Navel. "You are about to find out."

WE PREPARE FOR LANDING

IT WAS NEARLY a perfect takeoff in the single-engine seaplane. Celia did everything just as she remembered it from her show, except for one small thing. When she lifted the nose and the plane rose off the river at sixty miles per hour, she screamed long and loud, and so did everyone else on board. That didn't usually happen on *Love at 30,000 Feet.*

By the time they were done screaming they were airborne, rising over the twisting tributary of the Amazon. After a few wobbles and dips, Celia got the hang of flying. It wasn't so hard. She mostly just had to hold on to the controls and try not to move too much. All they had to do was stay close to the river and use it like a road to guide them.

"This will lead us right to where your parents

are," the llama girl said. "I do hope they are safe. Those loggers are a dangerous bunch."

"You guys are pretty dangerous too," said Celia.

"We're not dangerous at all!" the girl objected.

"Remember that little game of dodgeball?" Celia glared at her.

"Oh, that . . ." The girl scratched the back of her neck. "We don't get many visitors. Sorry."

"What's your name, by the way?" Celia asked. "I keep thinking of you as llama girl."

"Quinuama," she said. "It's an Inca name. You can just call me Qui."

"Qui," Celia said. "That's nice."

They flew for hours without saying much. Qui was enjoying the view from the sky. She had never been in an airplane before. Celia was getting kind of bored. She had spent too much time in airplanes.

The warriors in the back of the plane fell asleep and Oliver found himself being used as a pillow. They snored. There was no in-flight movie, which was the only thing Oliver liked about flying. He couldn't wait for this flight to be over.

And soon enough, it was.

"Over there," said Qui, pointing at a clearing on the banks of the river.

Two speedboats were tied up at the edge of a pier. There were a few buildings by the water, most of them ruined and overgrown with vines. An old factory had a tree growing through its roof. There was a rusty water tower and a narrow path through the jungle to another clearing on a hill. That's where they saw the rows and rows of ruined houses, and a main street with abandoned shops and a movie theater.

They also saw people outside one of the houses, burly loggers keeping watch over the street. There was a black Mercedes parked on the street too, which they immediately knew belonged to the mayor of Benjamin Constant.

The men scurried around on the ground and pointed up into the sky.

"They know we're here," Qui said. "We should have come at night."

"Too late now," said Celia, lining up the plane with the river below. "Prepare for landing." The warriors woke up and wiped drool from their faces. Oliver wiped it from his hair and glared up at them.

Celia pushed a lever forward and the plane dipped to the side.

"Ahhh!" everyone screamed.

She yanked the lever back into place and the plane went straight again. She tried another lever.

"Ahhh!" The plane dropped a hundred feet toward the water.

"Celia!" Oliver shouted. "Do you have any idea how to land this?"

"Don't bother me," she yelled back. "I'm trying to remember the right episode!" She stared at the gauges in front of her. "And make sure your tray tables are in the upright and locked position," she added. "Prepare for landing."

No one had any idea what she was talking about or how they were supposed to prepare for landing, but it did sound just like something a pilot would say.

As the plane shot over the river and streaked lower and lower toward the ruined town of Snack Cakeville, Oliver had the horrible realization that there were some things you couldn't learn from TV, and landing a plane was probably one of them.

34

WE TRY A DIFFERENT TRICK

THE FIRST PHASE of the Zanzibar Gambit was complete. Professor Rasmali-Greenberg and Dr. and Dr. Navel were able to sneak around the house collecting supplies without attracting the attention of the guards. They saw Sir Edmund and Principal Deaver walk off toward the old factory with the mayor of Benjamin Constant.

"Her hair looks just like Teddy Roosevelt's," Dr. Navel whispered.

"Shh," his wife told him.

They huddled together in the bedroom of the house before making their next move.

"Everyone understand what happens next?" Claire Navel asked.

"Not really," said the professor.

"Not really," said Dr. Navel.

"Just stick to the plan." She waved off their

worries with a casual flick of her wrist. "The Zanzibar Gambit never fails."

"All right," said Dr. Navel. "Let's do it."

Patrick the monkey dragged the sack of flour into the closet and shut the door. The professor squeezed his massive body into the steamer trunk.

"I do hope this works," he said. "It is terribly uncomfortable for a man of my size to travel like this. And I believe I have stained my tie."

"Don't worry, Professor, we'll have you out of there in no time. You can enjoy some snack cakes while you wait." She shut the lid on him and sat down on the trunk.

"We're going to keep Oliver and Celia safe," she said. "I swear."

"I trust you, Claire. I always have."

They were about to kiss when they were interrupted by the professor's muffled objections from inside the trunk.

"Can we stick to the plan, please? It's rather hot in here."

"Okay, here we go." Dr. Navel took the garden spade and tossed it through the window, shattering the glass. He and his wife stood against the wall on either side of the window so the guards couldn't see them from the outside. In the closet, the monkey screeched.

"Go around! Look inside!" one of the guards called from the yard. Once the guards had run around the house to come in through the front door, the Navels climbed outside and ducked below the windowsill.

"Phase two," Claire said, handing her husband a pile of rubber bands. They waited.

The Navels heard the front door open and the clomping of heavy boots. Three of the loggers burst into the bedroom. They saw the unconscious body of the man who had been guarding the closet. They saw the large trunk sitting in the middle of the room.

They heard another screech from the closet.

"Quiet in there!" one of them shouted, and pounded on the door.

Another screech.

He went to open the closet door.

"I wouldn't do that if I were you," said Principal Deaver as she strolled into the room. Sir Edmund leaned on the door frame and crossed his arms as if he were bored. Beverly scurried up next to him on her leash.

"Why don't you two stand up and drop the rubber bands," said the mayor of Benjamin Constant, standing behind the Navels in the yard outside and pointing a pistol at their backs.

"I assume the professor is in the trunk," called Sir Edmund.

"And a monkey with a sack of flour in the closet, yes?" sneered Principal Deaver as the Navels stood.

"His name is Patrick," stammered Claire Navel. "How did you—?"

"I spent my schoolgirl years in Zanzibar," answered Principal Deaver. "It'll take more than the old Gambit to get one over on us. Now, if you wouldn't mind putting your hands up in the air, it seems we will have to restrain you again until your children arrive. You are making this much more difficult than it needs to be."

"They'll never take you to El Dorado," said Claire Navel. "Never."

"They'll do what we ask in order to protect their parents. If they do not, you will be eliminated."

"You monsters!" the professor shouted from inside the trunk.

"Oh, Professor. After all my generosity to the Explorers Club over the years, you try to spear me in South America with that trap and now you are working with my enemy. Perhaps it's time for me to start my own club, with a more selective membership policy." Sir Edmund sat down on top of the trunk and snapped a padlock on it.

"We'll have to separate you two," he said. "Mr. Mayor, why don't you take Ogden over to the water tower and toss him in. We'll keep his wife here with us. Maybe we'll have a little chat with her. When the time comes, we'll . . . what is that?"

"What?" said Principal Deaver.

"What?" said the mayor of Benjamin Constant.

"*Qué*?" said the loggers.

They all followed Sir Edmund's gaze out the window to the sky above the tree line. A small airplane was flying straight at them, dropping lower and faster every second.

"What the—?" said the mayor. The high-pitched buzz of the engine grew louder and louder.

"Let's try the Tibetan Trick," Claire Navel whispered to her husband while everyone was distracted.

"What's that?"

"Push!" she shouted, and shoved the mayor while his back was turned. "Now run!"

The Navels split off in opposite directions, sprinting around the sides of the house.

"After them!" Sir Edmund shouted, but by then no one could hear him over the sound of the plane only a hundred feet away.

"Duck!" the principal yelled.

The plane smashed into the roof of the house, tearing a large gash in it and sending Sir Edmund, Principal Deaver, and the loggers diving away from falling debris. Beverly hissed and bolted out of the house. Patrick abandoned his sack of flour and scurried out of the wide-open roof.

The plane streaked across the row of houses and came down in the middle of the main street, though it didn't exactly land. Its pontoons tore off, and then it bounced back into the air once, twice, three times, showering the street with sparks with each bounce.

Finally on the ground, it was still racing forward. It slid past the empty shell of the drugstore and it shed a wing on the corner of the abandoned ice cream parlor. When the wing tore off, the plane spun like a top, racing toward the old movie theater at the end of the street.

It crashed right under the marquee, which had

lost almost all of the letters advertising the last movie ever shown there. Only *T* and *L* remained, improbably next to each other. There would be no time to ponder what word these letters might have once made, as the plane smashed through the ticket booth and slid a hundred feet into the theater, coming to a grinding halt amid a tangle of movie theater seats, individually packaged snack cakes, splintered wood, and broken glass. A thousand bats awoke from the ceiling of the theater, screeched wildly, and took flight. After the last bat flapped out, the plane's engine spluttered to a stop. Outside, the last letters on the marquee clanged to the ground. The dark theater was silent once more.

Inside the wrecked airplane, all was still.

35

WE MISSED MOVIE NIGHT

OLIVER'S VISION WOBBLED. Images faded in and out. He saw a window of a house growing larger and larger. His parents stood just outside it. He saw a street in a quiet neighborhood. He saw a drugstore and a movie theater. Was he going to see a movie? He felt like napping. He wondered who all these painted men piled on top of him were. He needed to rest. He'd ask Celia what had happened after he got some rest.

Celia's head was throbbing. She was staring at a torn movie screen. She was upside down. She was upside down on a seat in a movie theater. She sat upright and shook her head. There was daylight behind her. She turned and saw the terrible wreckage where the airplane had crashed into the theater. She remembered everything: she missed the river, she saw her parents being held at gunpoint, she smashed into the street beyond them and skidded right into this theater. She had crashed the plane. And her brother was inside!

She jumped out of her seat and scrambled toward the wreckage. When she reached the cockpit, she saw the girl, Qui, still strapped into the cockpit, looking wide-eyed ahead of her. There was a hole in the cockpit glass where Celia had flown right through when she'd slipped out of her seat belt. She had no idea why she wasn't cut to shreds.

"Are we on the ground?" said Qui.

"Yeah. Are you okay?"

"I think so." The girl smiled. "Seat belt."

Celia nodded and went around to the side of the plane. A whole wing was gone. She didn't remember that happening. Inside, she saw her brother, unconscious, lying underneath six Cozinheiro warriors. They were all sound asleep. *The Daytime Doctor* always told his guests they should never fall asleep after an accident in case they had a concussion. They might never wake up. She pounded on the metal door.

"Wake up!" she yelled. "Wake up now, Ollie!"

He didn't move.

She yanked on the door handle as hard as she could.

It didn't move either. The metal was bent and twisted. It was stuck. She tugged harder.

Nothing happened.

"Please wake up!" She pounded on it and pulled on it again and again until she was exhausted. She leaned against the door, resting her head on the metal, and she wept. "Please wake up . . . wake up . . . ," she whined.

"May I?" a voice behind her asked, resting a large hand on top of hers.

"Dad!" She turned and hugged him tightly.

"Hello, Celia," her mother said. Celia looked up at her, wiping the tears from her eyes.

"Hi," she said, still not sure she could trust her mother. "Are you going to poison-dart me?"

"No, honey. Never."

"Throw me out of an airplane? Drag me to Tibet?"

Their mother shook her head. "We're here to rescue you."

Celia considered this, then nodded and hugged her mother.

Dr. Navel yanked at the airplane door. One, two, three hard tugs and it came off in his hands.

"Did you see that?" He smiled and held the door up. "Did you see me rip the door off?"

"Very good, dear," his wife said.

Dr. Navel reached inside and pulled Oliver out of the wreckage. One of the warriors moaned and they all started to wake up, wriggling out from under each other and sliding out of the plane. Qui unbuckled herself and climbed out of the cockpit. Everyone gathered around Dr. Navel, who was holding his son in his arms.

"Oliver," Dr. Navel whispered. "Oliver, time to get up."

Oliver groaned.

"Oliver, you have to wake up."

There was no response.

"Oliver!" Celia shouted. "*Celebrity Whisk Warriors* has been canceled for a talk show about politics!"

"What?" Oliver shouted, springing to life. "Injustice!"

It took him a confused moment to figure out where he was and what was going on and why he had a big bump on his head and a ringing in his ears.

But then he saw his father and his mother and his sister all together, and he broke out into a broad smile.

He looked around the ruined old theater.

"I'm sorry this isn't much of a family movie night," their mom said.

Oliver hugged her tightly. "After Tibet, I was scared we'd never—"

"I know, honey." She hugged her son. "I'm sorry for what I put you guys through. It's almost over now."

Oliver wanted to believe his mother, but with his parents, nothing was ever that simple. They heard the loggers shouting out commands at each other as they ran toward the movie theater.

"You have to go," Qui told them. "The loggers have tied up their speedboats by the pier. You remember what the khipu said?"

"Not really," said Oliver. He bent down and picked up a cream-filled snack cake off the ground. He put it in his pocket. Celia raised her eyebrows at him. "What? It's in the wrapper!"

She shook her head at her brother and turned to Qui. "What will you do?"

"We will stay and fight," she said. "These men come into our land and steal the trees. It is time they learn from whom they are stealing. But do me one favor?"

"What's that?"

"When you find the real Corey Brandt, tell him he should have ended up with Lauren on *Sunset High*."

She handed Celia Corey Brandt's cell phone that the impostor had stolen. The last photos on it were of the real Corey Brant up in a giant redwood tree.

"I'll tell him that *you* think so," Celia said, and put the phone in her pocket. She hugged Qui, her first real friend who wasn't her brother or a character on television.

Oliver just rolled his eyes. What was it with girls and vampires?

"Thank you," Claire Navel said to Qui and to all the warriors. "And good luck."

"We do not need luck," said Qui. "We're protecting our home."

The Navels found the side door to the theater and slipped out as the warriors pulled their bows and spears and blowguns from the wreckage of the plane. For a second Celia felt bad for the loggers. They had no idea how much trouble they were in.

"The pier is just past the water tower," Claire Navel told her family, pointing up at the logo of Velma Sue's snack cakes smiling down over the jungle.

The Navels ran through the backyards of the strange town, ducking low and crawling under tangles of vines and thorny bushes. They reached the factory next to the water tower and saw, across a broad lawn, an old pier with a few speedboats tied to it. A few men stood guard, holding heavy clubs and sweating.

As they crouched by the edge of the factory, they heard screaming from behind them. They turned and saw all the loggers running down the main street toward the pier.

"Cannibals!" They were shouting and dropping their clubs and rifles as they ran. The men guarding the boats looked confused at first and then saw the painted warriors chasing the loggers down the street. They jumped into the speedboats and started the engines.

"Come back here!" the mayor of Benjamin

Constant yelled, running out into the street, waving his arms, but his men had already untied and sped off down the river. There was only one boat left. Principal Deaver chased the mayor outside. The mayor was still shouting after his men when she pointed behind him up the street. The mayor looked back and saw Qui and six painted warriors charging at them. The Navels watched the mayor and Oliver and Celia's middle school principal break into a sprint worthy of gym class and lock themselves into the mayor's black Mercedes.

"They aren't really cannibals, you know," Oliver told his parents.

"A myth can be more powerful than a spear," added Celia.

Dr. Navel winked at his wife. She reached out and squeezed his hand. A knowing glance passed between them: Oliver and Celia were becoming explorers in spite of themselves.

The Navels saw that the mayor's car was surrounded. Qui stood among the warriors and knocked gently on the car window. She saw the Navels hiding around the corner of the factory and she waved.

"You can go now!" she called out to them. The

monkey was making his way across the lawn, dragging the heavy trunk behind him. Beverly was perched peacefully on top. Oliver hated to admit it, but he was happy to see her.

The Navels rushed over to help the monkey with the trunk, and they all climbed onto the last boat.

Qui knocked on the car window again. The window came down slowly.

"Are you going to eat us?" squealed Principal Deaver.

Qui smiled. "We are going to play a game," she said. "I believe you are familiar with dodgeball?"

Dr. Navel started the boat engine and they pulled away from the pier.

"And where are we off to, Claire?" Dr. Navel smiled, reaching for the throttle.

"I think," said their mother, "that we should ask Oliver and Celia."

36

WE ARE WITHOUT A DOUBT

CELIA LOOKED AT OLIVER.

Oliver looked at Celia.

This was their chance. They could shrug and complain and offer no help and they'd get to go home and there'd be no more adventures and they wouldn't have to face the Corey Brandt impersonator or their old nemesis, Janice McDermott. They could watch television and argue with their father about attending the latest lecture on novelty hats in ancient Greece.

But that would mean that Janice would still be at large. And the real Corey Brandt would still be missing. No more *Agent Zero*. No more *Celebrity Adventurist*. No hope of a *Sunset High* reunion. And their mother would probably leave again. She would never give up her search for the Lost Library, and she would never stop trying to get the twins to fulfill their destiny.

There was only one thing to do.

They had to help their mother end this quest once and for all. That's how they would get their family back.

"Something about a sweet sea," said Oliver.

"And darkling waters," said Celia.

"Well, this is the Sweet Sea. That's what they used to call the Amazon, before the conquistadors renamed it," their mother said. "Is that it? Is that all they told you?"

"Um . . . ," said Celia. Her memory was not so good for things that weren't on television.

"The Sweet Sea forks into darkling waters," Oliver said, smiling as he remembered it. "Beyond the serpent's tongue and through weeping trees, where doubt itself bends toward a shadow, there the knight should boldly ride, if he seeks for El Dorado."

"How did you remember that?" Celia asked.

"You told me how." He smiled. "*Wally Worm's Word World.* You told me it was easier to remember a rhyme, like with *ossuary* and *gilded*. I just kind of remembered 'shadow' and 'El Dorado' . . . they rhyme."

"Sort of," grumbled Celia. She wished she'd been the one to remember it.

"Great job, Oliver!" said their mother.

Celia crossed her arms and leaned back as the boat sped forward. "I told him how to do it," she said.

"What do you think it means?" Dr. Navel asked his wife.

"Well, the weeping trees have to be rubber trees," she said. "When you cut them, they weep out rubber. But otherwise, I don't have any idea. Doubt doesn't bend."

"Maybe when you get more information, your doubt bends," Dr. Navel tried. That theory didn't make much sense.

"Doubt is the name of a river," Celia perked up. "The River of Doubt. Theodore Roosevelt discovered it. It's called the Roosevelt River now."

"Okay," said Oliver. "How do *you* know *that*?"

"Principal Deaver talked about it when you got us in trouble," she said with a smile.

"I didn't do it," Oliver muttered. "Beverly and Greg Angstura got us in trouble."

Beverly, still resting on the trunk, flicked her tongue.

"The River of Doubt!" both their parents exclaimed.

"If we take this branch of the Amazon to the River of Doubt," their father said, "and turn when it bends toward a shadow—"

"Away from the sun!" said Oliver.

"And see rubber trees," their father continued, "then we should find El Dorado!"

"Oh, Celia, well done!" said their mother, nearly knocking Celia over with a hug. Dr. Navel accelerated the boat, his glasses splattered with spray from the river. The monkey screeched with happiness. There was a loud cough from inside the trunk.

"Ah," said Dr. Navel. "Perhaps someone should let the professor out of the trunk now. I can't imagine he's comfortable in there."

It took a few minutes for Claire Navel to find tools on board the boat to cut the lock off of the trunk and a few more minutes to get Beverly to move from her spot without biting anyone.

"Professor," she said as she popped off the lock. "We have wonderful news. The work of the Mnemones is nearly complete!" She lifted the lid with an excited flourish, which quickly turned to disappointment.

Professor Rasmali-Greenberg was not in the trunk.

But Sir Edmund was.

And he was holding a blowgun.

"That *is* wonderful news!" said Sir Edmund, standing up. "Now, this is how one performs the Zanzibar Gambit!"

With that, he blew a large dart right into the back of Dr. Navel's neck.

"Not again," said Dr. Navel as he slumped, unconscious, over the steering wheel.

37

WE ARE SO OVER "IT"

THEIR MOTHER DOVE across the boat to catch her husband. She lowered him onto the seat, grabbed the wheel, and straightened the boat before they crashed into the thick mangrove roots on the banks of the river.

"Oh, I see you've rescued my lizard," said Sir Edmund as he climbed out of the trunk. "Thank you. As to the matter at hand, I have a supply of the antidote for the poison now coursing through your father's veins. I can happily provide you with it, *after* you take me to El Dorado."

"You don't even know that you'll find what you're after," their mother said. "The scholars at Alexandria destroyed the entire library to keep the Council from getting it. Why do you think they would have preserved it?"

"What is 'it'?" Celia asked, but no one answered her.

"Hold on," said Oliver. "I thought El Dorado was the City of Gold. Not libraries."

Sir Edmund chuckled. "The City of Gold refers to what it cost to build the place, not what it's made out of. Gold is a terrible building material. Trust me. . . . I once had a car made of gold. Terrible gas mileage."

"Janice McDermott and the fake Corey Brandt are already on their way there," said Oliver. "They could take everything before we get there."

"Oh, I'm sure I could work out some sort of deal with my old friend Janice." Sir Edmund sat and rested his blowgun across his lap.

"Okay," Celia demanded, "what is 'it'? What are we looking for? Why are explorers always so cryptic about everything?"

Their mother didn't answer; she just kept driving the boat. Sir Edmund ignored Celia's question and looked over at Patrick. "I see you have a new pet."

Patrick screeched at him and showed his teeth.

"Whatever." Celia crossed her arms angrily.

She didn't care what "it" was that they were looking for as long as they could all go home soon. She almost hoped Sir Edmund found it so this would be over with. The fate of the world couldn't really rest on something in an old library, right?

The boat sped on and none of them spoke. The forest formed an endless wall of green on both sides. As they drove, the color of the water grew darker. They saw the river split in two.

"Darkling waters!" Celia called out. The water on one side of the fork was darker and they followed it. As they drove through the winding river, caiman darted beneath the surface. Strange birds squawked and took flight. Their mother slowed the engine.

Straight ahead of them, they saw a giant tangle of branches and roots suspended over the middle of the river. Trees on each side of the water had grown toward each other and coiled together in the middle, supporting each other and growing up toward the sunlight. At their base, the roots created a mouth, with vines hanging down like fangs. The water flowed through it where a tongue would be.

Even Sir Edmund looked nervous as the boat passed through the mouth of the coiled trees. On both sides of the water, slashes in the rubber trees wept with milky goo and the river made a sharp bend into a dark cove.

Claire Navel pulled the boat into the shadows and pressed it up against the shore.

"I think we've arrived," she said.

"Let's go then," said Sir Edmund. "Everyone out."

"We can't just leave my husband here," she objected. "Mosquitoes will leave nothing but skin and bones."

"The poison in his veins will knock out any mosquito that bites him," said Sir Edmund. "Now let's go. We've got a Lost Library to find."

38

WE GET SUCKED IN

THEY CLIMBED OUT of the boat, leaving Dr. Navel, Beverly, and Patrick the monkey behind. Beverly tried to follow them, but Oliver put her back in the boat to keep watch over their father. He took the snack cake out of his pocket and left it with her so she'd stay. She perched above it like she was guarding an egg.

"Good girl," said Oliver.

"Don't forget who she belongs to," said Sir Edmund. "I intend to put her back in my zoo when this is over."

After a short but exhausting hike, they arrived at a pile of stones that was as tall as Oliver and overgrown with weeds. Just beyond it they saw another pile of stones, this one the size of a house and also overgrown with weeds. As they stepped past it, they saw the ruins, half a dozen flat-topped pyramids, tangled in jungle vines and plants, with large boulders and collapsed walls scattered between them. There were overgrown terraces and steps.

"Remind you of anywhere?" Sir Edmund asked Oliver and Celia. The place looked just like the ruins of Machu Picchu.

"Why are there always ruins?" Celia sighed.

Sir Edmund tore some of the weeds from the stones right in front of them and smiled brightly. He saw the key, the symbol of the Mnemones, carved into the rock. They wandered around the ruins for a while, studying the old stones.

"How do we get in?" asked Oliver. "There are no doors anywhere."

He and Celia sat on one of the crumbling piles of stones while Sir Edmund and their mother kept searching.

"We have to do something," said Oliver, slapping at a mosquito. He was hot and tired and worried. "We can't sit here all day."

"What can we do?" his sister replied.

"We always think of something."

"Never on purpose."

"Well, maybe if we tried . . . like explorers do."

"Oliver, all explorers ever do is nearly kill us."

"Okay," said Oliver. "So what would nearly kill us?"

Celia just shrugged.

"Come on, think!" Oliver pleaded. "We've been nearly killed hundreds of times!"

"I'm tired of thinking," said Celia. "I just unmasked an impostor of my favorite actor, flew an airplane over the Amazon, and found the Lost City of Gold! I'm done!" She stomped away from her brother.

"Celia!" he cried out. "You did it!"

"What?" she snapped, and turned back toward her brother, except she couldn't move. She was sinking. She was sinking in a pool of quicksand. "Oh, this is just great."

She crossed her arms and scowled. She would have tapped her foot, but she couldn't move it. She blew some hair out of her face. She stopped sinking.

"Panic!" Oliver shouted. Sir Edmund and their mother came running over. Celia was up to her ankles in the pool of quicksand. She glared at her brother. "Quicksand is only dangerous if you panic," Oliver explained. "Remember?"

Celia remembered. They saw this on *The Celebrity Adventurist.*

"What was Corey Brandt's First Rule of Adventuring?"

"I don't know," said Celia. "There were so many different ones."

"Don't panic!" Oliver said. "If you fall into quicksand, be sure to stay calm and still and you won't sink. The only way to sink into the quicksand is to panic."

"So you want me to sink?"

"Yes!" Oliver ran over to a tree and grabbed a vine and handed it to his sister. "Tie this around your waist. If this doesn't work, we can pull you out again."

"Oliver?" his mother asked. "What are you thinking?"

"I bet this quicksand is like a trapdoor," he told her. "Just like in our vision. The TV sank."

"Celia?" their mother asked.

"I think he's right." Celia sighed. "For once."

Their mother looked at both her children and nodded. Sir Edmund grumbled.

"This is why I hate going first," said Celia, and she started flailing around like Madam Mumu on

Dancing with My Impersonator. She sank quickly to her waist, then to her shoulders. "Here we go," she said, and shimmied one more time as much as she could in the thick slurry of sand.

She sank to her neck and then her chin. She took a deep breath and vanished below the surface. The vine kept sinking. It pulled and stretched. It strained. All was still.

Sir Edmund, Oliver, and Claire Navel watched the pit of quicksand and waited. Oliver and his mother held their breath.

"We have to pull her up," Oliver's mother said at last, grabbing the vine.

"Hold on!" Oliver stopped her. "Just another second."

"I know you and your sister argue sometimes," she told him. "But this is no way to get back at her!"

"It's not that," said Oliver. He pointed at the vine. It moved once. Twice. Three times. "That's the signal. She's safe!"

Just like in the old temple at Machu Picchu, Celia had sent the signal for the rest of them to come down. After some convincing, Sir Edmund went first. He climbed into the quicksand, grabbed on to the vine, and squirmed and flailed and danced his way underneath.

"If you tell anyone about my dancing," he said just before his face went under, "I'll—" He sank before he could finish his sentence. After they felt him tug three times, Oliver climbed into the quicksand. It seeped over his feet and locked around his ankles like a pair of wet socks.

"Mom," he said as he started to wiggle to make himself sink faster. "If we find the library, will you come home?"

She bent down. "I will always come home," she said, and kissed him on the forehead.

And then Oliver sank under the sand.

For a moment it was terrifying. The sand let in no light. All was dark and hot and wet. The pressure of the sludge pressed on his nose and mouth and eyes. It was like lying on the couch under too many blankets in the middle of summer. He worried he'd get stuck. He worried he would drown. He started to squirm and to panic for real.

And then it was over. He was hanging on the vine, soaked, a few feet above a stone floor, looking up at a dripping pool of sand from underneath.

He let go and dropped to the ground. Celia and

Sir Edmund were next to him. There was a dim flickering light coming from the other end of a long hallway. The walls were engraved with the symbol of the Mnemones. Oliver reached up and tugged the vine three times.

They watched their mother's feet appear from above, kicking and whirling in the air. Then her waist came into view and then the rest of her slid down, holding the vine until she was on the floor, as wet as the rest of them.

"Well, that was something you don't do every day." Claire Navel smiled. "Shall we?"

Oliver and Celia followed the two explorers down the hallway, running their hands across the smooth stone on the walls. They turned the corner and bumped right into their mother's back. She had stopped in her tracks and was staring upward.

They were on a balcony in a giant room with round walls that rose high above them and sank far below. The walls were covered in shelves, and each one was labeled in a strange language.

"Quechua," said their mother. "The language of the Inca. The Spanish outlawed it, but it survived. It's still spoken today."

Sir Edmund just snorted. He didn't care about linguistics.

Bridges and ramps cut across the space, connecting the shelves to each other, and large arched doorways opened into other chambers that looked just like the one they were in.

Stone stairways swirled along the walls, connecting the upper and lower shelves. Far below them was a pool of water that reflected the room back up at itself, creating an illusion that the space went down forever. The effect was dizzying.

Hundreds of fireflies flitted in the open air, flashing their lights. They were the only source of the light in the room. They cast an uneven, unending glow.

"So . . . ," Oliver said. "Is this the Lost Library?"

Although a writer might want to describe the space as "awe-inspiring in its vastness, infinite in its aspirations, the greatest feat of human ideas and engineering," Celia provided the most astute answer of the moment.

"Duh," she said.

"So where did all the stuff go?"

All the shelves in the vast space were empty.

"Someone got here before us," Sir Edmund gasped. "They took everything."

"Not everything," said Oliver, pointing.

On the opposite side of the room, leaning upright on a shelf was a single scroll.

39

WE ARE NOT TALKING ABOUT PLAY-DOH

THEIR MOTHER AND Sir Edmund looked across at the scroll, then at each other. They stood frozen for a moment and then both of them took off, sprinting in opposite directions, leaving Oliver and Celia dumbfounded. The two explorers raced around the library to get to the scroll, just like Oliver and Celia raced to get to the remote control.

Their mother would have won easily, but she tripped on a crumbling step and lost valuable time. They arrived at the scroll at the same moment and both of them grabbed for it. Oliver and Celia watched from a distance as Sir Edmund and their mother played an angry game of tug of war with the ancient document.

"Let go," muttered Sir Edmund. "You'll tear it."

"You'll never get it," said Claire Navel, trying to kick the little man away.

"Who could have stolen a whole library?" Oliver wondered as they watched. "Janice McDermott and the fake Corey Brandt?"

"They couldn't have done this," said Celia. "They were only a few hours ahead of us."

"What do you think that scroll is?" Oliver asked.

"I dunno," said Celia, "but I guess we should go help Mom."

"Stay right where you are!" a woman's voice demanded. They turned and saw Janice McDermott and the fake Corey Brandt standing right behind them. The celebrity impersonator had his gun pointed at them. "We never would have found our way in without your help," said Janice. "Thank you."

Oliver and Celia looked at each other. This is just what Janice's old partner, Frank, had done—tricked them into guiding him in Tibet and then left them to perish in a dark cave. They had outsmarted him and fed him to an abominable snowwoman. It was a pretty nasty situation and they would have preferred to forget all about it. That is the trouble with having enemies. Getting rid of them usually just makes more enemies. Anyway, there were no abominable snowpeople in the Amazon.

"And you two!" Janice called out. "Don't move or we'll shoot the children!"

Sir Edmund and their mother stopped tugging on the scroll and looked back toward the twins. They froze, but neither of them let go. Oliver and Celia went pale—paler than they already were. Why were people always threatening to kill them?

"Janice," Sir Edmund called out. "I have no quarrel with you. Shoot the children if you must, but perhaps we can work out a deal? I am willing to pay very handsomely for—"

"Ahh!" the fake Corey Brandt screamed, falling over into Janice. Oliver and Celia spun around to see what was happening.

"Beverly!" Oliver shouted as the lizard jumped onto the fake Corey Brandt's face.

"Run!" their mother shouted. Oliver and Celia bolted off toward their mother as she snatched the scroll from a distracted Sir Edmund.

"Hey!" he shouted as she raced toward her kids.

Sir Edmund tried to give chase, but shots rang out as the fake Corey Brandt fired at him. He ducked down and put his hands over his head. Their mother pulled Oliver and Celia down the stairs and into another large chamber.

"After them!" yelled Janice.

The impostor ran across a bridge and leaped onto the stairs below. He rushed through the archway into the next room and saw the Navels running up the stairs on the opposite side.

The giant room looked exactly like the one they had just left, with the empty shelves, the fireflies, and the reflecting pool at the bottom. The twins turned into another archway but slammed into a mirror.

"It's a trick," said Oliver. "This place is like a fun house."

"Some fun," said Celia. The mirror reflected the room back at itself and made it seem like it led into another giant chamber. There were dozens of archways all over the room, and now they didn't know which ones actually led to another room and which ones were illusions.

Corey fired his gun at them again. He missed,

but shattered the mirror. Behind it was a stone wall.

"That's bad luck!" shouted Oliver as they turned and ran across another bridge toward another opening into another giant room, identical to the others.

"What is this place?" Celia wondered.

"This way," their mother said, running up the stairs, searching for openings that might lead to a way out. Sometimes they ran into a mirror, sometimes they found another room. They popped out of one archway high above Sir Edmund, who was backing slowly away from Janice McDermott.

"I can help you get the Navels! I can help you avenge Frank Pfeffer!" he was saying. "No need to do something you can't take back. . . ."

Beverly came running along the wall to join the Navels. She was holding the snack cake Oliver had given her, still wrapped in its plastic.

"We have to rescue Sir Edmund," said Celia. "Then we can trade him the scroll for Dad's antidote."

"We can't let him get this scroll," their mother said.

"Seriously, Mom?" snapped Celia.

"What's so important about that scroll?" asked Oliver.

"Well, honey," their mother said. "This is Plato's Map."

"All this is about Play-Doh?" said Oliver, shocked.

"Plato." Celia rolled her eyes. "He was an ancient Greek philosopher."

"That's right," said their mother. "And he wrote the first description we have of the lost kingdom of—"

"Where'd you go, Navels?" the fake Corey Brandt shouted from below as he searched for them. They all ducked; even Beverly pressed her neck low against the floor.

"Mom? Oliver?" whispered Celia. "Maybe we can save the explanations for another time? We need to get out of here. Dad's still lying poisoned in the boat and we need to rescue Sir Edmund and get the antidote from him one way or another."

"Agreed," said their mother. "I'm just not sure how."

"I have an idea," said Oliver, gently taking the

snack cake from Beverly and tearing open the wrapper.

"I told you that's just a myth," said Celia.

"Myths have to come from somewhere," he said as he tossed the cake over the railing. Sir Edmund and Janice McDermott turned and watched it fall. It hit the water with a *plop*.

Then nothing happened.

"Told you," said Celia.

"Why are you throwing cakes?" Janice shouted. The fake Corey Brandt ran out onto the bridge below them, panting.

"Hey!" he shouted up.

He raised his pistol, but he never fired it. The room started to shake. The pool of water below bubbled and churned. Suddenly a spout of water shot straight up and smashed into the bridge, knocking the impersonator off his feet.

Another waterspout erupted and tore the bridge right off the wall. Soon, spouts were shooting from the water with the force of a hundred fire hoses, tearing off chunks of stairs and shattering mirrors. Janice fell over. The water started rising.

"Remind me not to let you eat those cakes anymore," their mother said. She tucked the scroll into her waistband, grabbed the twins' hands, and rushed back toward the way they came in. Sir Edmund ran after them.

"Wait for me!" he shouted.

"Come back here!" Janice called, trying to stand up. Another spout of water knocked her down again. The stairs behind Sir Edmund crumbled. They were crumbling faster than he could run.

"Help!" he called out, leaping into the air as the stone beneath him disappeared.

Celia was the first to react. She let go of her mother and dove back, catching Sir Edmund by the wrist. Oliver grabbed on to Celia around the waist so she didn't fall.

Oliver and Celia were sliding, unable to keep Sir Edmund up.

"Help!" Celia called out. Their mother grabbed on to her children and they all pulled Sir Edmund up together. He tried to snatch the scroll out of her waistband, but she slapped his hand away and pinned his arms behind his back.

"Let's go," she told Oliver and Celia as she dragged Sir Edmund down the hall they'd first

come through. Beverly raced ahead. The vine was still rising up through the quicksand and the lizard scurried up.

"Climb," their mother told them. Water was rushing down the hall and knocking into their legs, getting deeper by the second.

Celia caught Oliver to keep him from falling over.

"You go first," she said. This time Oliver didn't object. He grabbed the vine and climbed, holding his breath when he got to the sand and using all the strength he had left to hoist himself up through it. Celia followed him.

"And you," their mother said to Sir Edmund, wheeling around him once she saw her children were safe. "You'll give me that antidote right now."

"Give me the scroll."

"Give me the antidote!"

"We don't have time to argue," Sir Edmund shouted, already up to his waist in water. "Your husband will die if you leave me down here."

Claire Navel hesitated. She looked at Sir Edmund and then up at the way her children had gone. The water kept rising.

"Fine," she said at last. "But this isn't over."

"Of course it isn't." Sir Edmund sneered as he took the scroll with one hand. Claire snatched the antidote and climbed the vine.

Sir Edmund grabbed on behind her as the water filled the underground chamber.

There was no sign of the fake Corey Brandt or of Janice McDermott.

40

WE LOSE A FRIEND AND GAIN A FRIEND

WHEN THEIR MOTHER and Sir Edmund burst through the surface of the quicksand, Oliver and Celia were catching their breath on the ground. The sand bubbled as water churned in the space below. The children saw that Sir Edmund had the scroll.

"I'm sorry," said Oliver. "I'm sorry I destroyed the library and that you lost your Plato scroll."

"You saved us all, Oliver," their mother said. "You have nothing to apologize for."

Sir Edmund chuckled. Oliver ignored him.

"Now that the library is gone, though," he said, "will you come home?"

"Oh, that's priceless!" Sir Edmund laughed. He looked at their mother. "He thinks you'll come home. He thinks it's over!"

Oliver's mother glared at Sir Edmund. She turned back to Oliver.

"Honey, it's not just about the library," she said.

"What are you talking about?" Celia demanded.

The earth shook before she could answer.

"I don't think we should stay here," their mother said.

"You've got to come home!" said Oliver. "You said you would!"

The ground quaked and twisted, but Oliver and Celia stood, unmoving, staring at their mother.

"Guys," she said. "I will come home, I promise, but—"

"There's always a but, isn't there?" Sir Edmund laughed. "A big but!"

The ground shook and knocked him off his feet. He fell backward into the pool of quicksand. "Help! Help!" he shouted, flailing his arms, the scroll waving in the air above his head.

Celia glanced at her mother and her brother and then at Sir Edmund. She rushed over to him and snatched the scroll from his hands.

"Hey! You clurb't derble—," he spluttered, his mouth filling with quicksand as he tried to grab Celia, making himself sink deeper.

"You better stop moving or you'll drown," said Celia. Sir Edmund had sunk up to his mustache. His eyes blazed with anger, but he stayed still and stopped sinking. Then Celia turned to her mother and showed her the scroll.

"Now you'll come home," Celia commanded, and marched toward the boat. Her mother knew better than to argue, so she followed.

Suddenly, with a giant sucking sound, the largest of the ruins of El Dorado disappeared before their eyes. Then the ruins next to it disappeared, and then the one next to that. All the ruins were falling into giant sinkholes, churning with mud and stone and water. Sir Edmund gurgled in the quicksand but didn't dare move.

"Maybe we should—," Oliver started when a sinkhole opened right in front of him. "Ahh!"

He flailed his arms in the air, falling forward toward the roiling water deep below. Celia caught him just before he plummeted into the abyss.

"Thanks," he said, looking back at the disappearing ruins and then at the puddle of quicksand. "We can't just leave Sir Edmund to die," he said.

As much as she hated to do it, Celia agreed.

Leaving Sir Edmund was the kind of thing he would do to them, not the other way around.

Their mother nodded.

"Oliver," she said. "Do you still know your knots?"

"I do," said Oliver.

"Then tie up his wrists," she told him, tearing off a strand of vines. Oliver did as he was told. Only when his wrists were tied did they pull Sir Edmund from the quicksand.

"You no-good, lousy, rotten—," he started the moment his mouth was free, but all three of them gave him a look that told him to keep his mouth shut or they'd dump him back into the quicksand. Just to be sure, they used some moss and another piece of a vine to gag him so he couldn't talk. The rage in his eyes told them everything he was thinking.

Then they all ran, stumbling toward the river as the ground swallowed the ruins of El Dorado and the Lost Library, leaving nothing but muddy pools in their place. Trees tumbled as their branches and vines were caught in the sinkholes. Angry birds took flight.

They jumped into the boat, tossing Sir Edmund

on top of the trunk as if he were a sack of potatoes. Celia gave the antidote to their father, who woke up with a groan. When he saw his wife and children, and Sir Edmund tied up, he smiled and hugged his children. He kissed his wife deeply.

"Gross," said Oliver.

"I found it, Oggie," said Claire Navel, holding up the scroll. "Plato's Map!"

"Plato's Map!" their father cheered. "You mean *that's* what this was about? I didn't even think that existed."

"No one did," said Claire Navel.

"You did. You knew," said their father. "And you were right."

"Oh, honey." She smiled as she broke the wax seal on the scroll and began to open it. "I'm always right."

Sir Edmund rolled his eyes. Dr. Navel leaned over his wife's shoulder to see. Oliver and Celia sat with Beverly and Patrick and watched from across the boat as their parents looked at the scroll.

"But—," said their father. Their mother went pale. She dropped the scroll onto the floor of the boat and leaped back onto the shore.

"Honey, wait!" said Dr. Navel, running after

her. He turned back to Oliver and Celia. "Kids, stay here. We'll be right back." Oliver and Celia watched their parents race into the jungle.

"What . . . what just happened?" wondered Oliver.

Celia got up and scooped the unrolled papyrus from the floor of the boat. She studied it and sat back on the trunk.

"It's not a map," she said. "It's a note."

She turned it so Oliver could see. There was no map, just a note in the middle of the page.

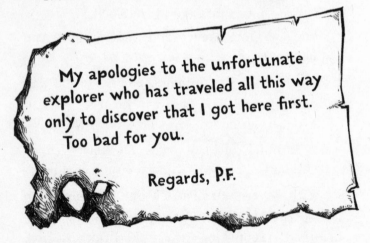

My apologies to the unfortunate explorer who has traveled all this way only to discover that I got here first. Too bad for you.

Regards, P.F.

"Who's P.F.?" Oliver wondered.

Celia shrugged. She looked over at Sir Edmund. He looked as surprised as their mother had.

Oliver scanned the jungle for their parents. The trees shook and animals fled in all directions. After what seemed like an eternity, their father came back . . . alone.

"Where's Mom?" Celia asked.

"She . . ." Their father looked sadly at the jungle. "She won't be joining us," he said, jumping back into the boat.

"What?" both children demanded.

"She's sorry," he told them. He looked as upset as they were. "She wants me to take you home. . . . She says she's got to look for clues. She can't stop now."

Oliver looked one more time at the jungle.

"Now you see what your mother really cares about," Sir Edmund snarled at them, spitting the mossy gag out of his mouth.

"Are you behind this note, Edmund?" Dr. Navel demanded.

"Of course I am," he answered sarcastically. "I trekked all the way through the jungle and got poison-darted by your wife and shot at and nearly drowned so I could look at a smart-aleck note from an unknown explorer and let your wife get a head start looking for the real thing while I'm tied up with you!"

"No need to be so rude," said Dr. Navel. "She did give me something for you." He pulled out a piece of paper and held it in front of the little man's face. "Read it out loud," he commanded.

"I, Sir Edmund S. Titheltorpe-Schmidt the Third, forgive all debts owed by Oliver and Celia Navel—," he started. "Hey! I do no such thing!"

Dr. Navel shrugged and reached for the blowgun that Sir Edmund had used on him earlier.

"Well now, Navel, calm down," he stammered. "Violence never solved anything. . . . Okay . . . okay." He kept reading. "They are hereby freed and absolved of service to me from this day forward from now and forever. They may also keep my lizard, if they so choose."

Oliver was surprised to find himself happy about that. He'd grown to like Beverly.

"Sign it," said Dr. Navel, pulling a pen from his pocket and shoving it into Sir Edmund's mouth. Sir Edmund grumbled but did his best to sign the paper.

"I didn't want the lizard back anyway." He spat the pen out and glared at Oliver. "You ruined her."

Beverly hissed at him. Oliver ignored him. He was looking back at the jungle. Celia rested her hand on his shoulder, and he clenched his jaw, fighting back emotion.

"She won't be coming, Oliver," said Sir Edmund. "She still believes she can beat me."

"I think she just did," said Dr. Navel, picking up the blowgun.

"Now, Navel, don't do anything rash. I set them free. . . . I'm sure we can—"

He fainted before Dr. Navel could even shoot the dart.

"Well, at least we'll have some quiet time together," Dr. Navel said as he started the boat. Oliver and Celia looked sadly at each other. "I'm sure Mom will come home soon," their father told them, although he didn't even sound like he believed it. "You guys can tell me what I missed."

All three of them looked back at the jungle one more time and then their father eased the boat onto the river and back toward civilization.

41

WE ARE PRESENTED WITH A PRESENT

"**THANKFULLY, I REMEMBERED** Corey Brandt's First Rule of Adventuring," Corey Brandt told the interviewer, with a wink and his trademark smile.

"Which rule is it this time?" Oliver rolled his eyes.

"Shh," snapped Celia, turning the volume up on *Celebrity Access Tonight*.

"We've watched every interview he's done. That's like three hundred by now. And it's a different rule every time."

Celia pressed pause and froze the image on the screen so she could be more threatening when she glared at her brother. Cable television was truly magical.

"I don't see *you* surviving stuck in a tree for two weeks."

"All he had to do was not fall," Oliver complained. "We were the ones who had to have all that . . . *adventure*." Oliver said the word *adventure* the way you might say *boogers*.

Celia hit play again. "Always count on your fans," Corey Brandt continued.

"Seriously? Come on!" Oliver tried to grab the remote from his sister. Patrick the monkey sat on top of the refrigerator and clapped. Apparently, he loved a good wrestling match. Beverly, back in Dr. Navel's favorite armchair, flicked her tongue. She flicked her tongue at most things these days. She hardly ever hissed anymore, ever since Sir Edmund disowned her. As lizards went, she wasn't the worst.

It had been almost four months since their adventure in the Amazon. Oliver and Celia spent the last two days of their school suspension using the photos on Corey Brandt's cell phone to find exactly where the teen star had been trapped.

Dr. Navel couldn't believe it when his children begged to go with him to the giant redwood forest in Northern California.

"You know," he told them, "giant redwoods sprout copies of themselves from their own branches, duplicating themselves over and over again . . . sort of like impersonators."

"Whatever," said Oliver and Celia. They just couldn't wait to meet the *real* Corey Brandt at last. They didn't want to learn about trees.

When they found the teen star, he had lashed himself to a tree branch and was delirious from hunger and thirst. He was dreaming about a big Italian feast.

"Noodles," he said, and passed out in Dr. Navel's arms. The teardrop freckle was under his eye, just where it was supposed to be.

After his rescue, he told everyone the most exciting tale of Janice and the impersonator's diabolical plot to trap him in a tree and take his place. And he described how the Navel twins and their father had rescued him.

"Oliver and Celia Navel are the true adventurists," he said. "And I am honored to call them my friends."

When Oliver and Celia came back to school, it was like their first day had never happened. Even the eighth-grade girls wanted to watch *Fashion*

Force Five with Celia. All the boys wanted to be just like Oliver. He was the first picked for every team, even though he was terrible at every sport.

They never had to play dodgeball again.

Principal Deaver had not returned to school. Their new principal was friendly, honest, and most decidedly *not* an explorer. She did, however, bear an amazing resemblance to former president William Howard Taft.

Mr. Rondon, too, was gone, and the new custodian didn't know exactly what had become of him. There were rumors he had gone to South America to live with a tribe of cannibals.

The twins made it to Christmas vacation without anything else exciting happening to them. They missed their mother, but they were thrilled to know that they could watch cable TV over the break and didn't have to be slaves to Sir Edmund. Their father promised they wouldn't have to go anywhere exotic or do anything interesting.

"I cannot, like, wait to join the Explorers Club myself," Corey Brandt told the interviewer on TV. "I have just pledged all the money from my latest prime-time special to protect the indigenous people of the Javari Valley in Brazil from outside intruders. I love, you know, doing good. Activism is, like, so . . . you know—"

Their father stepped in front of the screen and turned it off.

"Hey!" Celia objected. "We were watching that!"

"You'll have plenty of time to spend with Corey Brandt when he comes to visit for the New Year's banquet. Now, it's time for dinner."

"But—," Oliver started to ask just as Professor Rasmali-Greenberg came in. He was wearing his red and green tie where all the ducks wore Santa Claus hats.

"Merry Christmas!" he said. "Happy Hanukkah. Good Diwali!"

"It's none of those holidays," said Celia. "Christmas Eve isn't even until tomorrow."

"Ah, ever since Sir Edmund and his cronies resigned from the Explorers Club, every day feels like Christmas to me!" The professor laughed.

"Cronies?" Oliver wondered.

"Oh, just look it up yourself," Celia answered him.

"I hear they have started a new club," Dr. Navel said.

"Yes, the Gentlemen's Adventuring Society," said the professor. "I fear the Council will be far more open with their work now that your wife has thrown down the gauntlet, so to speak. We have no idea who this P.F. is, but rumor has it that your wife is interrogating scholars of ancient Greek history from Athens to Fiji."

"Rumors," said Dr. Navel, glancing at Oliver and Celia. "Just rumors."

"Pardon me," said the professor. "The holidays are no time for such talk."

Oliver and Celia looked at each other. Since they last saw their mother, she hadn't so much as sent them a postcard. During the journey back home, they had told their father everything they knew about the history of the Mnemones and the Council. They told him about the prophecy that the oracle had given them in Tibet and what they'd seen in their vision in the jungle. They even told him about the catalog of the Lost Library in their remote control. Their father was at times shocked, at times amused, and always very impressed with the daring young children he had raised.

But he shocked them himself when he told them to forget about all of it and just watch TV.

He got them cable the day they arrived back at the club. He wanted them to have a normal life, he said, just like he and Claire had discussed when they were trapped in the closet in Snack Cakeville.

And for the past few months, things had been totally normal. Boring even. It was great. This was the first time they had heard anything about their mother in all that time.

"The holidays are a time for presents!" the professor exclaimed, and ran out into the hallway, knocking the moon rock off its shelf. He came back with a wrapped box. "This is for you both to share," he told Oliver and Celia. Dr. Navel looked at him curiously as he stepped into the hall to put the moon rock back.

Oliver reached out for the present, but Celia got to it first and tore the wrapping paper off. Oliver's shoulders slumped.

"A new backpack," he said.

From his seat on top of the fridge, Patrick the monkey studied the new backpack carefully. Beverly flicked her tongue.

"Look inside," said the professor, smiling.

"Two wet suits," said Celia, pulling out the

thick black scuba-diving suits. "And a book." Her shoulders slumped.

"Professor, what's this about?" asked Dr. Navel nervously.

"That's the complete works of Plato!" The professor smiled. "In translation, of course . . . but it's not from me. Open it."

Celia opened the book and saw that it was inscribed to Celia and Oliver.

"Mom!" she said, recognizing the handwriting immediately.

"Claire!" Dr. Navel exclaimed and almost jumped over the couch to see what his wife had written.

"Dear Celia and Oliver," Celia read out loud. "I know you hate doing reading during vacation, but I think you'll find that your remote control comes in handy here. You might want to learn what the scholars of Alexandria knew about Plato. Enjoy the rest of sixth grade. I'll see you both *very, very* soon. With love, Mom."

Celia set the book down on the table. The apartment was silent for a long time.

"Well," their father said at last. "I think things

have been normal around here for about long enough."

"Oh no," said Oliver.

"Oh no," said Celia.

"Why don't we have a look at that catalog in your remote and see what your mother wants us to know?"

"I thought you wanted us to have a normal life," Celia objected.

"Oh, Celia." Their father sat down between his children. "Normal is so dull, isn't it?" He smiled widely.

"Dinner's getting cold!" Oliver tried.

Dr. Navel ignored him and picked up the remote. "Now, how do we work this thing?" He started hitting buttons.

"That's not it!" said Celia.

"She doesn't know!" said Oliver.

They both reached for it.

"Hold on, I think I know," said their father as he struggled to keep his children from wrestling the remote from him.

To the people watching from a rooftop across the street, dressed in black and bundled against the cold, it almost looked like innocent family fun.

But they knew better.

Two of them held binoculars to their eyes.

"Let me see," the third one whined, pushing a wisp of nearly perfect brown hair from his eyes. "You wouldn't even know about the remote if it weren't for me hanging out with those kids!"

"And you would still be half drowned in the Amazon if it weren't for me coming back to rescue you," snapped Sir Edmund.

"Shh," said Janice McDermott. "I need to read their lips."

"Why do you need silence to read lips?" said Sir Edmund.

"I have to concentrate," she snapped.

"Then we have a deal?" Sir Edmund said. "You'll have your revenge."

"Oh yes," said Janice. "And you'll have your library."

"I just want one thing from it." Sir Edmund smiled. "And that alone is more than you can possibly imagine."

"Whatever," said Janice, who didn't really like all the cryptic explorer talk. Why were they so mysterious about things all the time? She preferred the company of grave robbers.

"What are they saying?" nagged the fake Corey Brandt, whose real name turned out to be Ernest.

Sir Edmund lifted the binoculars back to his eyes.

Through the window across the street, he saw Oliver and Celia Navel let go of the remote control as Dr. Navel pointed at the screen. The professor leaned on the couch behind them and muttered some nonsense that Sir Edmund couldn't make out. But he watched happily as the twins rolled their eyes and their father excitedly mouthed one word:

Atlantis.

"Merry Christmas, Edmund," Janice said to him with a smile.

"And to you too, Janice," he answered her. "Very merry indeed."

A NOTE FROM THE AUTHOR

THERE ARE A FEW POINTS I feel the need to clarify before we see Oliver and Celia Navel again on their next adventure.

First, you should be relieved to know that the practice of cannibalism, which was never widespread in the Amazon, is all but extinct. As our friend Qui explained earlier, tales of cannibals were often used by European explorers to excuse their own brutish behavior while they ripped through the Amazon rain forest, stole its resources, and enslaved its inhabitants. Tales of cannibals were often completely made up for no other reason than to sell books!

While the Cozinheiros are an invention of mine, there are indeed at least seventy uncontacted tribes in the Brazilian Amazon. Their way of life, which may seem strange to us, adds great richness to the ethnosphere—which the real-life explorer-in-residence at National Geographic, Wade Davis, describes as "the sum total of all thoughts, dreams, ideas, beliefs, myths, intuitions, and inspirations brought into being by the human imagination since the dawn of consciousness." Or as Dr. Navel put it, "from the Songlines of the Aboriginal Australians to celebrity dance competitions."

While we outsiders might think it would be good to bring uncontacted tribes into our society so they could have things like flu medicine and celebrity dance competitions, like all peoples, they have a right to determine their own destiny and to choose if and when they would like to reach out to the world beyond the forest.

These tribes do have occasional and sometimes deadly encounters with other societies around them and their land is indeed threatened by illegal logging and mining operations. Unlike Qui's tribe in this book, most do not emerge as victors from these encounters. Their personal loss is a tragedy and the destruction of the ethnosphere is an ongoing catastrophe. You can learn more about the challenges that indigenous people around the world are facing and how you can help from Survival International at http://www.survivalinter national.org.

The khipu are real. The Inca created untold numbers of these knotted string bundles and they were used to carry information throughout their empire. However, no one has yet figured out what they mean, and indeed, the Spanish destroyed most of the ones they found when they first conquered South America. The Museum of Natural History in New York City has a wonderful collection of 124 khipu, although only five are on display to the public at this time. It will take a lot more research to crack their code and decipher their mysteries. It will take some vision too.

As for Teddy Roosevelt's expedition, he did actually navigate the River of Doubt with his son Kermit in 1919, and the expedition nearly cost him his life. As far as anyone knows, he did not stumble onto El Dorado, or any other lost city.

Snack Cakeville is not a real place, but it is based on Fordlandia, which is, unbelievably, a real place—a model American town built in the heart of the Amazon by the carmaker Henry Ford. Like

Snack Cakeville, his experiment was a failure, and the town has largely fallen into ruin, reclaimed by the jungle and forgotten by history.

Did that answer your questions?

I hope not.

The act of exploration is an act of continual questioning, and unlike Oliver and Celia, I hope you will be curious to learn more about the people and places we encountered in *We Dine with Cannibals*. As Marcel Proust wrote, "The real voyage of discovery consists not in seeking new landscapes, but in having new eyes."

I hope you will share with us what you see.

Please visit http://www.calexanderlondon.com to share your discoveries, questions, and ideas, or write us an old-fashioned letter at:

C. Alexander London
Explorer, Adventurer, Librarian
Care of: Philomel Books
345 Hudson Street
New York, NY 10014 USA

ABOUT THE AUTHOR

C. ALEXANDER LONDON is an award-winning author of nonfiction for grown-ups, an accomplished skeet shooter, a master scuba diver, and a fully licensed librarian. He has watched television in twenty-three countries and survived an erupting volcano, a hurricane, four civil wars, and a mysterious bite on his little toe in the jungles of Thailand. Currently, C. Alexander London lives in Brooklyn, New York.

www.calexanderlondon.com